# THE CRIME, THE PLACE, AND THE GIRL

# THE CRIME, THE PLACE, AND THE GIRL

DOUGLAS AND DOROTHY STAPLETON

COACHWHIP PUBLICATIONS
Greenville, Ohio

*The Crime, The Place, and The Girl*, by D. & D. Stapleton


Cover image: Janaka Maharage Dharmasena

First published 1955
Douglas Stapleton, 1907-1972
Dorothy Stapleton, 1917-1970
CoachwhipBooks.com

ISBN 1-61646-573-5
ISBN-13 978-1-61646-573-5

# 1

The gremlins that were playing crokinole inside Peter Hack's skull made a particularly vicious carom shot, and Peter winced.

Jacob Tobias, his boss, grunted with fierce satisfaction. "So maybe you've got a conscience after all. Five hundred dollars from petty cash—and you don't remember how you spent it. Make faces all you like, like Boris Karloff, even."

Peter Hack straddled the chair back, thrusting his legs an amazing distance in front of him. He laid long, gangling arms along the back of the chair and glared at his boss. He reached up and shoved his excellent but battered hat farther back on his head—not to be picturesque and typically a newshound, but for the strictly utilitarian purpose of rubbing his head. It was a furtive rubbing that had nothing to do with conscience. He was merely exploring to see if any of those carom shots were actually coming through his skull.

"All right. So I'm a liar and a cheat and a thief! Sure. I lied all over the lot about this Great Opus of yours. Loeb Films, I told Louella, has produced the greatest, most heart-warming film to come out of Hollywood since 'Broken Blossoms.' And that makes me a liar. Confidentially, Jake, 'The Clock Struck Three' stinks."

Jacob Tobias, the stout, usually amiable and always voluble president of Loeb Films, opened his fat, babyish lips in wild protest. Pete, however, flagged him down with one large flapping hand.

"And I cheated all right. I cheated about seven years off Marilyn's age. And not her legal age at that."

Jacob made vague gestures, as if he regretted having brought down on himself this deluge of words and would like to get out from under. Peter Hack stabbed at him with a lean and bony forefinger. "And as for thief . . . sure, I'm a thief. I stole more newspaper space for 'The Clock Struck Three' than they gave to 'The Robe.'" Pete could have gone on for some time in this vein—and he would have enjoyed it.

Jacob Tobias looked actively unhappy. But that was not unusual. Jake had two expressions—actively unhappy and exuberant. There was no middle ground for the little producer. He was made up of extremes, and this was one of his lower moments. He held up a fat, pudgy hand, reminding Pete vaguely of a comedy traffic cop. "Now, Pete, you shouldn't take these things so serious. It's only I should want to account to Alwyn Phillips for five hundred dollars out of petty cash. Besides, what's petty about five hundred dollars—to a banker, anyhow?"

"What does a New York banker know about show business—except to look at a girl's legs? Not that I think Phillips has the nerve even to do that. He's a mouse—a mouse that walks like a man."

"He is also representing the Alwyn money, Pete. And the Alwyn money owns Loeb Films. Well, almost. So just try can you remember what you did with the five hundred, so I can put it on the books." Jake was almost pleading with his public relations man. "Just try . . ."

Pete honestly tried. It was all very vague, but pleasant. An evening in Hollywood, holding the ear of the working press, mostly by pouring something down its collective throat, was likely to turn out somewhat vague. He remembered Louella all right. And Jim Meadows of INS. And Bellew. . . . And there his memory trailed off into a kaleidoscope of the Brown Derby, the Trocadero, Maxie's, Mike's and a little dark cellar place somebody said had a terrific boogie-woogie pianist. As Pete recalled, the somebody had been right about the boogie-woogie pianist—but there recollection stopped. Pete decided on diversionary tactics. "Look at your morning spreads. More space than . . ."

Jacob sighed. "I know. More space than 'The Robe' got. That much I like. But I still gotta show Phillips the books on 'The Clock Struck Three'—and how do I charge the five hundred?"

"Charge it to experience." Pete grinned wryly. "Put it on première expenses. Or overhead."

"We got too much overhead. That's why Phillips is here, snooping in the books. And the première . . ." Tobias sighed regretfully, as only a man with a guilty conscience can sigh.

Pete knew the reason for the sigh. Jake, with an artist's fine disregard for money, flung it happily away creating pictures. But always came the awful day when the producer had to add up the books and present an accounting. With "The Clock Struck Three" completed, in the can, edited and ready for its world-shaking première, Jake was beginning to feel the effects of his artistic binge.

Seeing the stricken face, Pete managed to divert some of his own self-pity. Tobias had spent more than a million dollars to produce "The Clock Struck Three," and within hours the fate of that million—and the picture—would be decided before Hollywood columnists and critics. Now Tobias was having the artistic shakes. He always had them after finishing a picture and before the public had passed judgment on his latest work. This time the artistic shakes were aggravated by Alwyn Phillips, New York banker, who had come out to supervise the spending of the Alwyn money invested in Loeb Films. Because of those jitters Jake was having a fight with his ace publicity man over a mere five hundred bucks. Of course, Pete realized, if it hadn't been over the five hundred it would have been a fight over something. Tobias had to let off steam and Pete was his safety valve.

Right now the safety valve was nursing a million-dollar super-colossal production of a hangover and he wanted out. Peter wanted coffee—quantities of coffee—a triple bromide and eight hours of sleep. He suspected he might get the coffee and the triple bromide. Sleep was out of the question. The première of "The Clock Struck Three" was less than four hours off, complete with newsreel cameras, stars in evening clothes, floodlight, announcers, red carpets—Jake's fling at reviving an old and once valued tradition, a real night of glory. So it had to be good. And so had "The Clock Struck Three." It was up to Pete to see that the mechanics of the première were at least smoothly functioning, sufficiently glamorous and adequately liquid.

Despite his crack, Pete considered "The Clock Struck Three" the best of Jake's many successes. It wasn't, in itself, splashy, like the première. It was essentially a simple story—the love, spats and reconciliations of just ordinary people—but touched with the Tobias artistry. It was so good that even Marilyn Courtney looked convincing as a sweet and somewhat shy young wife. It was so good it might even save Charles Abbott from the oblivion into which he was threatening to slide—deservedly, Pete thought. If it is true that no man is a hero to his valet, then it is doubly true that no star is a hero to his press agent. Pete didn't like Abbott and he had his own private reasons.

He did like his boss and his job with Loeb Films, so Pete slid his hat back to a perilously insecure angle and stood up. "Take the five hundred out of my salary. Mark it 'advance' and forget Phillips."

"Now, Pete . . ." Tobias looked hurt. "I should take it out of your salary? For a measly little five hundred dollars?" He sank down behind the vast expanse of desk and waved Pete away. "I'll think of something."

"Don't worry about my salary, Jake. I'll get it back on my next swindle sheet. And we must keep dear Alwyn happy. Once the grosses start to pile up . . ."

Jake slid unhappily deeper into his chair, until his round pink face was only visible, like a setting moon, above the rim of the desk. The moon shook sideways. "No, Pete. This is my last picture. I know it. Pete, I am a no-good failure. I should maybe have stuck to the tailoring business, Pete—if I had ever been in the tailoring business." Jake sighed. "I got an uncle in Brooklyn, Pete. He's got a nice business. A tailor shop. . . ."

Pete knew that plaint and he was as familiar with that uncle's tailor shop as if he'd been brought up in it, even though he considered it at least partially fictitious. Reminiscences about life in a tailor shop invariably marked the low point in Jacob Tobias' self-esteem. To Pete it meant the turning point. This was the nadir. Below this Jake would not go. From now on the swing would be upward until, after a successful première or an even reasonably pleasant première, Jake would be irresponsible again—and well launched into his next venture.

Pete closed the door gently on a view of Jake's round, despairing face.

His next view of Jacob Tobias was from between bobbing heads and above several mink-covered shoulders. Jake had started his upward climb again. He was just at the becomingly modest stage as he received the more important guests at his première.

Pete elbowed his way around to the newsreel man and the two Loeb Films cameramen who were covering the entrances of celebrities from the top of a sound truck nosed into one side of the theaters broad outer lobby. He scrambled up the narrow ladder and edged himself perilously among the twisting snakes of cables and crouching men until he reached a point where he could survey the red carpet, the gold ropes that held back mere onlookers and the hand mike a sound man was desperately thrusting between Jake and someone Pete hoped was Spencer Tracy. Joe, the sound mixer, craned his head out of the truck cab, reached up and tugged at Pete's trouser cuff.

"For goshsake, Pete, didn't you give Jake but one speech? It's getting so I think my sound track is stuck. A plug for your lousy show is all right, but he's overdoing it."

"The show's swell. You can't overdo it. And anyhow, you can cut out Jake's greetings. It's the stars the public want to see—and hear."

From his vantage point Pete watched the pageant he had so painstakingly staged. The studio police, well trained, were keeping the crowd back—but not too much. The stars would have been bitterly disappointed if an occasional fan hadn't broken through to pant up with book and pen held out. He pointed one out to the Loeb Films cameraman. "Get a shot of that kid breaking through. They'll eat it up. Catch one every now and then."

Pete pointed out the shot he wanted and settled back to watch the show. To Pete, this was the show. What went on on the screen inside didn't count. Pete was satisfied. Marilyn Courtney dodged out of her limousine and was neatly blocked by an autograph hound, right in front of the camera. Marilyn made a pretty scene of gay acquiescence and bent over the kid's book, giving the camera just the right amount of profile. And the kid was properly awestruck. Pete made a mental note to jack the kid's pay five bucks.

He made a swell little stooge. Now the kid was worming his way back into the crowd, proudly holding up the autograph book. Pete sneaked a look to see if the newsreel men had gotten it. They had.

Corliss Petry, Loeb Films featured player, and one Pete strongly suspected would get an Oscar for her work in "The Clock Struck Three," smiled at the crowd, waved up at Pete and went on into the theater without trying to hog a few extra feet of film. Corliss was Pete's special pet and he, along with most of the men and women on the Loeb lot, adored the middle-aged, gracious character woman. Charles Abbott, looking excessively boyish and charming, grinned his way past a group of girls beyond the rope, turned back to sign an autograph book hurriedly. One of the girls flung her arms around his neck, pulled his head down and kissed him soundly. Abbott straightened, confused, and backed away as the others tried commando tactics to get through the rope lines. Studio police closed in efficiently. Swell stuff—exactly as Pete had rehearsed it.

Robert Emery, Loeb Films character man, got caught in the final swirl and was almost carried across the rope before a studio cop recognized him and set him back on the carpet. That was good, too, even if Pete hadn't dreamed it up. He grinned down at Emery straightening his bashed-in homburg. So you want to be a matinee idol?

Emery waved his hat, sighed and went over to shake hands with Jake, and Pete hoped the little producer would remember his speech for Emery. Pete had taken considerable care with it and wanted it recorded for posterity—well, at least a week of posterity. From the speed with which Emery left to enter the theater Pete knew Jake had muffed it.

When he turned back the cameramen were chuckling and aiming their cameras at a wildly gesticulating girl who was being thrust back into the crowd beyond the ropes.

Pete frowned slightly. He hadn't staged that particular demonstration and he didn't recognize the taut, tragic face turned up to him just before the crowd closed in around her. It was a haunting face and it kept recurring to him. There was something more than tragedy in it.

Tom Brady, Loeb Films' Western Star, pranced by like one of his horses, to wild whoops and cheers from the crowd. Brady, in dress suit, sombrero and cowhand boots, was a picturesque enough figure on his own, so Pete had not bothered with a stunt. For another reason, too. Pete seriously doubted that the amiable oaf could have carried it off successfully.

And then it was over, at least Pete's part. He climbed stiffly from the sound truck and invited the cameramen to the press party. With their cans of film shot off to labs by messenger, the cameramen were open to suggestion. Pete guided them as far as the door and shoved them into the hazy, smoke-filled press room. Then he went off into the quiet darkness of Jake's private projection room where he knew the producer would later be viewing the rushes on the night's take of his première. Now, however, Pete had two hours, maybe more, before "The Clock Struck Three" would grind to its genial, tender, sentimental end, and Jake would be prodding him awake. . . .

Jake was prodding him awake, jubilant, bubbling with plans for his next picture. "An Academy Award for sure," Jake chortled. "Even Charles Abbott looks like an actor. Next we do . . . Pete, ain't you listening?" He turned back to the slender, elegant figure in the darkened projection room. "Mister Phillips, we got an Academy Award picture—and he ain't listening!"

Pete blinked awake and stared. The première must have been a success to make Jake actually jovial with Phillips. However, the New York banker squelched the little producer's enthusiasm. "I can scarcely accept the judgment of that crowd, Mister Tobias. It was hand-picked for favorable reaction. However, the picture did strike me as acceptable."

Pete unfolded from the comfortable depths of one of Jake's lounge chairs and stood up. "The rushes of the newsreel shots should be ready, Mister Tobias." Pete could be as coldly formal as Phillips. "Shall I tell the operator to begin?"

Startled at formality from Pete, Jake nodded and sat, his fat legs thrust childishly in front of him, his plump fingers drumming a happy tattoo on the arms of the chair.

Pete pressed the button that would signal the operator. There was a whirring click and the projector started with a blinding flare of light. Somewhere off beyond Jake, Pete could sense Phillips sitting in frigid dignity, waiting for the re-enactment of the night's première. The screen darkened. Once more Marilyn Courtney was properly cordial, Corliss Petry was gracious, and Abbott fumbled correctly. Emery got caught in the backwash of Abbott's phony popularity. Then Alwyn Phillips stalked awkwardly before the camera and passed on. Pete hadn't remembered his entrance, but then, at premières, bankers weren't important. And then the camera swung to the unscheduled performance.

The screen showed the press of people against the gold rope—and a girl who fought her way through. She got to the rope and began to climb over. A cop caught her arm and thrust her back. And then, for an instant, her face was turned full into the camera. It was a thin face, and might even have been attractive, but now it was twisted with terror, etched with desperation. Full sensitive lips were screaming to someone out of camera range. The cop was thrusting aggressively, and the girl stumbled back into the crowd, her shoulders and head craning wildly toward the camera, fear and panic in her eyes. Then the crowd closed around her, swallowed her up. The camera flashed to Tom Brady. At least it should have been Tom next. Pete never got a chance to see who it was because Jake was shaking him.

"Pete! That girl! She's terrific. She's marvelous! I never seen such emotion, such fear. Pete, you hear me?"

Pete nodded in the darkness and then, realizing Jake couldn't see him, added, "Sure I hear you."

"I want that girl!"

# 2

"Like a bolt from the blue, Tobias recognizes talent! Boy!" Jake swiveled himself in his chair and yelled at the soundproofed projection booth without effect. "Boy! Run that shot over again!"

Pete plucked the hand mike from its nest in the arm of Jake's special chair and held it up. Jake grabbed the mike and settled back. "Run that part over that shows the girl busting out of the crowd. Two-three times, maybe."

The screen went black, then glaring white. Jake squirmed around to face Pete. "Don't you even know her name? You hire maybe a future Bette Davis for ten bucks and don't ask her name? Such efficiency! And for that I pay you five thousand a week!"

At the mention of this entirely fictitious salary Pete saw Phillips stiffen and then glance at him with sudden new respect.

The screen darkened and once more they were seeing Marilyn graciously signing an autograph book. Pete watched closely this time, right from the start. In early sequences—just as Corliss passed—he had detected a surge of movement on the outer fringes of the crowd. Through the shot of Abbott being kissed he traced the course of the disturbance, caught by the undiscriminating, undistracted eye of the camera. Emery got his hat knocked off, grinned at the camera and passed. Pete caught a glimpse of the frantic figure thrusting closer to the rope. Alwyn Phillips' precise profile blocked the view for an instant and then—the girl.

It was obvious she was trying to reach someone beyond the range of the camera. Pete studied her. The face was probably oval in repose. Now her mouth was open and the lines of her cheeks drawn thin and long, with a hungry, pinched look—and her eyes, despite the glaring floodlight, were open wide—and enormous.

Somewhere in there Tom Brady loped across the screen, but Pete's attention was focused on the upper left corner. The studio cop blocked the view, so that only the girl's frightened, strained face showed above his shoulder. She was screaming a protest, pleading with the man—and being inexorably thrust back into the crowd. Her handbag slid from under her arm and swung out on its strap heavily. The stout, matronly woman next to her got banged on the elbow with the bag and turned to glare, rubbing her arm indignantly and saying something to the cop. The man on the girl's other side closed in, thrusting the girl back, until only her enormous, frightened eyes peered over his shoulder. A slight sidewise movement cleared her face for one last glimpse, and Pete saw desperation and then hopeless, bottomless despair, before the girl turned back into the crowd and was lost again, except for a slow surge of movement that marked her going.

Jake's long-drawn, satisfied sigh called him back to the moment—and Jake's intentions. "Such talent! Such drama! Like I direct it myself! Tears, even. Tears standing in her eyes! With a scene like that I tear their hearts out. I have her waiting. On a dock, maybe. A ship is coming in. No, going out. On it is her sweetheart. She must reach him. And then—the crowd, the rope, the cop. She gets there—

too late! Everything is lost! Tears in her eyes, sobs in her throat, ache in her heart—she turns away." Overcome by his own powers of description, Jake sniffled. He drew out a large handkerchief and blew his nose. "Of course, for the happy ending he comes back, they are happy and have six children."

That was Jake's formula for happiness—six children. So far he had achieved only five but, since they were neither all girls, like Cantor's, nor all boys, like Bing's, they had little publicity value and Pete had ignored them as much as it is possible to ignore a boss' adored offspring.

"Pete, I want that girl!"

Offhand Pete could have given him a dozen reasons why he couldn't get her—not the least of which was that Pete hadn't the vaguest idea who she was—and another dozen reasons why, if he could get her, she wouldn't measure up to her one brief performance. And it was a good performance, Pete granted that—if it was a performance. But somehow, he was developing a sneaking suspicion, it wasn't a performance. That terror and despair were the real goods. For his money, that let her out as an actress. He could also point out they hadn't heard her voice, which could be anything from a high, irritating whine to a low whiskey rumble. However, he was saved from presenting his arguments. Phillips was doing it for him.

". . . And furthermore, I've read of these attempts to build an unknown into a star. Very costly—and quite possibly the public doesn't like the star once she's created."

The little producer swiveled away from Phillips, ignoring the thin, precise voice. "I want that girl, Pete. We'll make from her a star."

Phillips' voice squeaked to an abrupt stop and he stood up, his arms jerking angrily, like a badly articulated puppet as he loomed above them. "I may not be able to avert this wildly chimerical and extravagant idea at the moment. But once I am in control, I'll see that these mad expenditures stop. There is a method of producing anything, motion pictures as well as any other commodity, that is sane and businesslike." The man clapped his homburg on at a rakishly defiant angle, the first impulsive gesture Pete had ever seen the meticulous banker make. "And I'll see that Loeb Films is run by strict business methods, once I'm in control."

Jake turned from Pete for an instant and looked up at the man. "And how many people should you kill?"

Phillips gasped and snatched off his hat as if it had suddenly become too hot for his head. "Mister Tobias," he almost choked, "I demand an explanation."

Jake blinked solemnly at Pete. "Tell him it's a joke, Pete. Tell him in Hollywood it's a standing joke you got to kill so many relatives before you get control."

Pete, with equal solemnity, relayed the information to Phillips who had undoubtedly heard Jake's version. He began a watery smile and bowed a little stiffly. "I'm sorry. I'm afraid I haven't got quite used to Hollywood levity. In my circles such an accusation is serious."

"Hollywood isn't a circle; it's a merry-go-round," Pete told him, and tried to concentrate on what Jake was saying about finding the girl. But something was distracting him. At first he thought it was his own plans for a campaign, suddenly conceived. Then he tried to lay it on Phillips' fidgeting, when he realized the blinker by Jake's chair was flashing. That meant a phone call. And who the devil—Pete squinted at his wrist watch—would be calling the studio at twelve-thirty? He nudged Jake and pointed.

The little producer clawed down and came up with the handset of his phone. "Yeah. . . . Yeah. . . . Sure. This is Jacob Tobias, head of Loeb Films. . . ." He twinkled gravely over the phone at Phillips. "For a while yet, anyhow." Then Tobias blinked and started nodding gravely to the telephone's muted squawking. He glanced at Pete in puzzlement, shrugged and resumed his nodding, as if the other person could see his agreement. Finally he spoke. "Never heard of him." Jake scowled perplexedly at Pete. "We got a actor named Derwent?" He pulled the phone up to babyish lips again. "That his real name or . . ."

Pete reached for the phone, sighing. "We've got him." He plucked the instrument out of Jake's hand. "What's he done now?" He glared at the squawking phone. "Police? No, we won't put up bail. It's past midnight now and . . ."

"Brother," stated the phone with tinny insistence, "where he's gone they don't give bail. And who are you anyhow?"

"Bill Katon! My ex-corporal!" Pete hunched deeper into the comfort of the chair and flung one leg over the arm. "This is Pete Hack. And what's Ed Derwent done this time?"

"Say, Pete, I'da called you first if I'd known what bar you were in. But Fels says get the Old Man himself, so I done it. And Derwent ain't done anything, and ain't likely to do anything. He's slightly dead. He died of somebody not liking him too much. Know him, Pete?"

"Some." Pete sat a little straighter, his voice cautious. "He's an extra we use around here once in a while. So somebody bumped off Derwent, eh? Well, we knew him slightly. Good-looking, but a nasty piece of work."

"Well," Bill Katon's voice dropped confidentially, "he's not good-looking any more, unless you admire 'em with an extra hole in the head. Fels wants him identified, Pete. Can you come around? We're at Derwent's bungalow on . . ."

"Why me? You know who he is. Say, why'd you call Loeb Films?"

"A guy named Kelley, Dan Kelley, found the body and called us. Said they'd just worked in a picture together. Something about a clock."

"Kelley?" Pete scowled at the phone. "Kelley at Derwent's? Why, he and . . ." Pete remembered the last time he'd seen Dan Kelley and Edgar Derwent together—fighting. "I didn't know they were friends," he covered hastily.

"Yeah, they worked together in 'The Clock Struck Three,' on location." He settled back in the chair. "Can't identification wait until morning? Or how about relatives?"

"Doesn't have any. And you know Fels. He wants to clear this up. He's got the murderer tagged—witness, everything. Come on up and identify the guy, so we can go to bed."

"Who did it?"

"Some dame. I don't know her name, but Fels has it sewed up. Be a good boy, Pete, and come along. The quicker we clean this the quicker I get to bed. My feet . . ."

"Okay, okay! I'll be there, Bill. What's the address again?" Bill Katon gave it to him and Pete hung up, turning to Jake. "Derwent got bumped off." But Tobias was gazing raptly at the screen that was reenacting, for perhaps the fourth time, the scene of the première. Once again the girl burst from the crowd, stared wildly into the camera and then vanished.

"Look, Jake, how's this? I get blow-ups of the girl from the film, plaster 'em all over every newspaper in Los Angeles . . ."

"In the country," amended Jake.

"With the caption, 'Jacob Tobias, motion picture producer says, "I Want That Girl!"'"

"How can you sit there, calmly discussing a publicity stunt," Phillips thrust himself angrily between them, "when a man has been shot to death? I should think you would be . . ."

"Be what?" Pete glared up at the banker outlined against the screen. "Want me to go up there and hold his hand? It's a little late for that. And Bynum Fels needs my help like he needs a third leg. He's got the murderer tagged. Even got a witness. Katon told me. Some woman killed him. It's cut and dried. So sit down—or go home."

"Oh!" Phillips subsided slowly. "I'm sorry. I guess I'm not used to the Hollywood attitude. You take make-believe so seriously, and you practically ignore a real-life murder. Did you say that a woman killed him?"

"That's what Katon said. Probably some poor kid he promised a screen career. That was a trick of his. Derwent, if you want to know, was a heel."

"I see." Phillips nodded slowly, and when he spoke again it was with his usual superior tone. "It's a relief to find that someone in Hollywood is businesslike and efficient. I imagine even the New York police couldn't do better—arresting the murderer within three or four hours of the murder."

Pete accepted the backhanded compliment in behalf of the Los Angeles police with a mockingly gracious nod. "I'll tell Fels you approve. It'll make him so happy."

Phillips coughed deprecatingly. "Oh, I wouldn't, if I were you. He doesn't know me. I think I'll go now. There's no point in keeping the car any longer." The banker turned a smug, complacent back on them, stalked down the aisle and let himself out.

As the door whooshed back on pneumatic hinges, Pete shook his head. "Of all the conceited nincompoops, that guy takes the prize. And I bet he even rented the car to go to the première."

"He did—and put it on the studio expense account." Jake made a childish but expressive noise. "Bankers I don't like. And him special. I should live to see him control Loeb Films."

"Can he? Ever?"

"If Amelia Alwyn dies—and changes her will." Jake managed to get the chronology slightly reversed, but Pete straightened it out mentally. "Which ain't likely to happen." That wasn't clear. Did Jake consider it improbable Alwyn would die or unlikely that she'd change her will? Jake clarified, "Amelia is supposed to be dying right now, but she's always supposed to be dying. She's too mean to die—and too stubborn to change her will." So Jake meant both, only Pete wasn't interested. He wanted to get the hunt for the new star launched.

"Look, Jake," Pete cut across Jake's volubility. "I've got to get out those prints if I'm going to make the late morning editions."

Half an hour later Pete sat hunched behind the wheel of his car, driving out to Derwent's bungalow, grimly cheerful in the thought that he had launched a campaign for a new star with just the sort of Cinderella motif the newspapers love. He was comfortably aware that most of the morning papers would carry a photograph of an unknown girl, and Loeb Films and Jake Tobias would share honors with an unknown, haunted face.

# 3

Bill Katon's face had all the homely efficiency of a bulldozer. It fed him through a broad and slightly lopsided mouth. It provided him with air through a nose that had never been beautiful and which three years as a not-too-successful boxer had not improved. And it provided a beetling retreat for his bland, cherubic eyes. But it was a face Pete liked to look at.

Bill turned and stared with Pete at the men moving in and out. "Sure is different from out yonder, isn't it? Make a big fuss over just one guy dying— and him a rat, from all I hear." Bill cocked his head and peered at Pete. "Or is he a friend of yours?" Which, from Bill, was remarkable tact.

"I knew him. Rat fitted him pretty well. Come on; let's get this over with." Pete and Bill moved off across the courtyard which the real estate agent had undoubtedly referred to as a patio. "Though I don't see why some of the neighbors couldn't identify him. They probably knew him better than I did."

Bill shrugged. "You know Fels. Sticks by the book. And the book says a close relative or last employer has gotta identify the corpse. You're his last employer, so you get the honors. Actor, wasn't he?"

"I've heard directors who denied it emphatically, but roughly it fits. Who're Fels' prize witness and suspect? Or is he being cagey again?"

"A gal named Germaine Winters. . . ."

Pete stopped and swore softly, thrusting his hat to the back of his head. "A thing like this shouldn't happen to a mess sergeant! Derwent of Loeb killed, Kelley of Loeb finds body, Germaine Winters of Loeb arrested for murder! Why didn't they do it on the lot and make a production of it! What the newspaper'll do with that!"

Bill grunted and stopped short. "You got it wrong, Loot. This Germaine is a dish—a lulu." Bill gave a low but expressive whistle. "And anyway, she's only a witness. Say, is she an actress in the movies?"

Bill's homely face, lighted harshly from the splash of light through the open door, held a dull, pleading look that Pete tried to interpret correctly. "Well, Bill, not exactly. . . ." The relief told Pete in which direction he could safely go. "She's Dick Hammond's assistant. He's casting director. Why?"

Bill started toward the "scene of the crime," muttering, "Just wondered, Loot. If she was an actress, she wouldn't pay any attention to a cop. But if she's just somebody's assistant, how can she afford to five in a swell dump like this?"

Pete glanced around at the shoddy grandeur of the typical bungalow court and felt briefly sorry that Bill thought this was "a swell dump." Or that Bill should think Germaine was a lulu. As he recalled her, she was a brassy blonde who had probably looked cute as kittens at seventeen and was trying now to forget the intervening dozen years and additional twenty pounds. For Bill's comfort he added, "Oh, there's a ceiling on these places. Sometimes girls team up."

Bill shouldered his way past several men, his head nodding complacent acceptance of Pete's solution. Pete followed him into the room. Shades had been removed from table and floor lamps—shades that had once mercifully shadowed the cheap finery—and the room blazed with fight. It was difficult to tell how much of the confusion and disorder was the result of the crime and how much was due to the swift thoroughness of Fels' Homicide Squad. Gradually, however, he sorted out the pieces. The opened drawers of the almost Spanish desk and the spewing papers were probably the work of the criminal. Even Fels wouldn't have searched that violently. The scuffed rug might be anybody's work, but the shattered lamp and the bottle on its side on the floor, both carefully outlined in chalk, had been there when the police had arrived. And Pete suspected that the man who was industriously picking up photographs sprayed across the room was gathering evidence, not straightening disorder caused by police. The chalked outline by the almost Spanish desk, grotesquely suggesting a collapsed scarecrow, was definitely police work. Pete glanced around for another outline and didn't see it. No murder weapon?

He peered at the incongruous piece in the phony luxury of the room—a case of guns, apparently war trophies, near the desk, and an open rack with one empty gap. Did that represent the source of the murder weapon? He shrugged and glanced again at the chalked scarecrow outline.

"Looking for something?" Bynum Fels' drawling, cultured voice was irritatingly superior.

"Yeah." Pete didn't even look up. "A body. I was supposed to identify one."

"Oh!" Fels chuckled. "I'm sorry. The M.E. took it down to the morgue. He couldn't wait. You picture people seem to think you own Los Angeles." The drawl was missing now, drowned in a querulous tone. "And I'm here to tell you you don't!"

Pete glanced up from his study of the floor and eyed Fels. The man was perhaps half an inch shorter than Pete but he looked taller than Pete's six feet because his shoulders were narrow and his head thin and faintly pointed.

He carried himself cockily on the balls of his feet, as if he were constantly trying to assure the world—and himself—that he was confident and alert. His face was thin and long and his eyes were deep-set on either side of a nose that, with a little more virility, might have been hawkish. As it was it was merely too large and too thin. The mouth was precise and coldly chiseled under a surprisingly virile moustache. The moustache twitched in anticipation of words, and Pete held up his hand. "I know. You're here to tell us movie people we don't own Los Angeles. That's interesting, because I thought you were here to solve a murder."

Fels flushed angrily and then patted his breast pocket as if he had the murderer dehydrated, rolled up and thrust there. "I've already solved it."

It wasn't sound practice, but the man irritated Pete, so he couldn't help it. "I suppose it's suicide while of unsound mind again." It was a reference to a case Fels had handled years before—and passed as a suicide. Pete, then a reporter, had covered—and broken the case as murder.

Two spots crimsoned high on Fels' cheeks and he turned and stalked off, his glazed pumps chopping precise steps across the rug.

"You shouldn'ta done that, Loot. He's sensitive."

Pete grinned and followed the cop with the armload of photographs into an adjoining bedroom-cum-study. More papers and photographs strewn across the rug, and an opened and thoroughly rifled file cabinet, indicated a hasty, frantic search. The cop glanced up at Pete as he dumped the load from the living room on the desk. "Fels says sort these tonight. Why, I'll be here three days from now." He slumped into the desk chair and slapped the papers into a rough pile, glaring at them. He paused, staring. Slowly he reached into the pile and jerked out an 8 X 10 print, whistling. He winked at Pete. "Maybe this ain't such a bad job after all. Blackmail's always tough, but you sure learn things!" He held up the photo for Pete's inspection.

The face had been scratched away so that only a white blob suggested where it had been. But the rest was clear—abundantly clear. And recognizable. Pete had seen that photo before—with a face. He knew the face, and so did perhaps thirty million other Americans. Marilyn Courtney's face had once leered drunkenly out of the photograph. Pete knew. He had bought the negative and "all" prints for five thousand dollars. The go-between had been a ratty little man with grimy hands and a turtle head that bobbed restlessly above a large and very dirty stiff collar. As the studio publicity man, it had been Pete's job to clear up the mess before the blackmailer ruined a million-dollar investment. And at last he'd come to the source—Derwent. If it had been that picture alone, Pete wouldn't have been so sure, but the cop was avidly turning over the other photos, hissing tonelessly through a gap in his teeth, and Pete knew Derwent had a thorough blackmail mill in that pile.

Pete wandered down a short hall to a bedroom. He suspected that a large portion of the five thousand he had paid for Marilyn's art work had gone into furnishing the gaudy and somewhat frilly room. It had the specious extravagance of an old-time deMille boudoir, with satin-textured walls, a taffeta-covered chaise longue and an enormous canopied bed with quilted silk headboard. The closet and a severely modern chest of drawers—the only piece Pete liked—had been as thoroughly rifled as the desk and file cabinet. The murderer had certainly been looking for something. Pete wondered vaguely if he'd found it. He corrected that mentally—if she had found it. Bill Katon had said Fels had arrested a woman. Pete started out, wondering why he had instinctively thought of a man as the searcher.

He turned back and studied the room. It was something about the closet. Under the disarranged suits, their pockets turned out, sat an orderly row of shoes. It was the combination that had given him the idea.

Women, he had heard somewhere, hid things in shoes. If a woman were looking for something small, such as a note or a photograph, she'd look inside shoes—and those weren't disturbed. On the other hand a man turned pockets inside out when he was hunting something. It was nebulous and negative reasoning, and certainly not a clue. Anyway, he wasn't looking for clues. He had nothing to do with the case except to point to a dead and repulsive face and say, "That's Edgar Derwent," and step out. For that matter, a "case" scarcely existed. Fels already had his murderer. Pete shrugged and went back to the living room.

Bill Katon was there, sitting placid and unperturbed in a Provençal chair that managed not to clash with the almost Spanish desk. Even with his feet stacked one over the other in the exact middle of the chalked, scarecrow outline, Bill was placid and unperturbed. "Where's Fels?" Pete asked.

"Snooping for more evidence against the dame." Bill jerked a thumb toward the half-open drawer of the desk. "Though from what I seen, she done the world a favor."

"Where's Germaine?" As Bill scowled Pete added, "The girl who witnessed . . ." and then realized he didn't need to identify Germaine to Bill. Something else was causing the scowl.

"Fels is holding her. Material witness. It's a dirty shame—a nice girl like her mixed up in a murder, just because she happened to see . . ."

"I mean, where is she now? And Dan Kelley, the guy who found the body, where's he?" Pete thought that over for a moment, sensing a discrepancy, but a curiously distorted painting of a most unappetizing nude had caught his eye. There was something in what he'd said, but for the life of him he couldn't pin it down for staring at the dazzling radiations from the nude's over-prominent navel. He walked over to the nude—a reproduction—and studied it. They weren't radiations and it wasn't a navel. The radiations were accidental, fine lines of shattered glass around a small neat hole, a bullet hole.

Pete lifted the picture away from the wall and peered behind it. There was a neat matching hole in the plaster. He dropped the picture back into place and looked back at the chalked outline and Bill's feet. In a line? Then he remembered what had troubled him. "Look, Bill, if Germaine witnessed the murder, how'd it happen Dan Kelley found the body?" If his head were only clearer this would no doubt be simple. Right now it seemed a problem.

"Yeah! That's right." Bill lunged to his feet. "Say, he's holding that girl illegitimately!"

Pete grinned. "Maybe we better talk to her."

"Yeah!" Bill lumbered to the door. "She's in her own cottage. Poor kid! Likely she's alone and scared half to death. . . ." Bill shoved his way through the door as if it had personally affronted him, and shouldered his way through a group of men scrambling to their feet. Pete followed him before he realized the men were reporters, and then it was too late. He could only hope they'd think he was another of Fels' men.

Then somebody hailed him. "Pete! You trying to hush this up for Loeb Films?"

Pete waved into the dark toward the voice. He grinned. "After that, could I?"

Somebody laughed. "Or are you going to out-sleuth that fellow Fels and fell the felon? Say, that's not bad, if I could remember how it went."

The wizened, dried-butternut face of Squidge Hanson poked up at him out of the dark, eyes wrinkling malevolently.

Pete hurried on, trying to catch up with Bill. He joined him just as the big man was rapping with surprising gentleness on the door of the next-but-one bungalow. Noises inside, a radio blaring and a blur of voices, indicated the timid knock went unheard. Pete leaned around Bills shoulder and pushed the bell. Inside, a two-toned chime bing-bonged. Someone said, “Cheese it, the cops,” and somebody else laughed and added, “The joint’s raided. See who it is and tell ’em we don’t want any.”

Behind that bungalow, or the next—Pete couldn’t tell which—a car started with an angry whirr of wheels spurting gravel. Wondering if he had missed Fels, Pete stepped to the corner and peered down the alley. A car shot briefly through a stream of light. It wasn’t a discreetly dark, official car. It was a roadster, long, low and blatantly yellow, that swung out of the alley, and started for town. It was gone in an instant, but Pete had recognized it. He’d gotten it out of hock at traffic court often enough to know it.

It was Marilyn Courtney’s personal car.

# 4

Pete glanced at Bill to see if he had noticed the car. Bill wasn't noticing anything but the girl who swayed in the doorway, saying huskily, "Well, are you coming in, or are you a memorial to something or other?"

While Bill was digesting this greeting Pete peered back at the reporters. There wasn't any disturbance there, so maybe they hadn't noticed. The game of crap, he thought, is a wonderful institution. Then he discovered he was being introduced to Germaine Winters, who waved a tall glass unsteadily at them. "Come on in. . . . Come in, Pete. . . . Get him a drink, Dan—and one for Gargantua."

Dan Kelley was struggling out of the depths of an extremely modern chair, trying not to upset a drink balanced on the arm. He made it with a lurch and straightened broad shoulders belligerently, as if he were angry with the chair. That was one of the things that made Dan Kelley a good actor—he could look perpetually angry. And it would probably keep him a character actor all his life. Dan Kelley played toughs—not tender-hearted toughs like John Hodiak and Humphrey Bogart—just toughs. "Hi, Pete. Join the mourners." He waved an arm around the room. "You know Sally." Sally was one of Loeb Films' minor starlets, at the moment taking a sip from some man's drink. She choked a little and said "Hi!" without looking up. The man wiggled the glass in a small salute when Dan said, "Carter Brainerd." He didn't look like a man named Carter Brainerd. He looked Irish and hard and as if he ought to be known in the ring as "Round House McGinty." Pete found out later he was named Carter Brainerd and came from Virginia, had three college degrees, a voice as smooth as Southern Comfort, and about three million dollars.

There was somebody else moving around in the kitchenette, and Dan flapped a hand in that direction. "Virginia Struthers. Beautiful." He peered at Pete and then at Bill, scowling. "That man's a cop. He arrested me. He arrested me and Germaine and my friends." His eyes swung back to Pete. "And I suppose you're here to protect the fair name of Loeb Films."

"Something like that, Dan." Leaving Bill with Germaine, who was trying to give him a sip from her glass, Pete walked over to Kelley's chair and sat on the arm. "Sit down, Dan. It makes me tired to see people stand up, and I'm already tired." Dan reached down to protect his drink and sat craning his neck to peer up at Pete.

"Can I help it if a guy gets knocked off just when I'm going to see an old pal?" He was more than a little drunk, and his belligerence had slurred over into sullenness.

"Ed Derwent wasn't your pal. The last time I saw you, you were . . ."

"You don't have to broadcast it." Dan said it low, harshly, scowling across at Bill.

"He wouldn't notice a herd of polka-dot elephants dancing the samba through here right now. . . ." Pete aimed a thumb at Germaine.

"Like that, huh?" Dan grinned wisely and took a long swallow of his drink and set it down. "Incidentally, that's what we were scrapping about. Derwent was trying to move in on me, in that nasty way of his. I wouldn'ta minded most guys trying to muscle in on me. I can hold my own with the rest of 'em. . . . But that guy . . ."

"Then how come you were out here and found the body?"

Dan shrugged. "It was one of those things. . . . Derwent invited us for a party—a champagne party, mind you. He was feeling keen—in that gruesomely gleeful way of his. He kept hinting something big was coming his way, so it was champagne." Dan took another swallow, sloshed it around in his mouth as if rinsing out the taste of saying the guy's name. "Free champagne from that guy? It sounded too good. I shoulda known something was screwy. Why, that heel wouldn'ta treated to salted peanuts in a free lunch. But it sounded good at the time. . . . Anyway, I had almost forgotten it until we were coming from the première. . . . Stopped in a couple of bars."

"Could you prove that?"

Dan Kelley jerked in the chair and looked up, his ugly, scowling face perplexed. "You think I'll need to? Pete, you mean it's serious?" Dan Kelley rubbed the back of his hand across his nose in a small-boy gesture of perplexity. "You know, I've played so many tough roles and seen so many phony murders that I can't get the right focus on this. I almost expect Tobias to come roaring in asking for retakes."

"It's serious, Dan . . . but Fels has his murderer. So you're out of that. It's the studio I'm thinking of. A good alibi would keep your nose clean."

Dan fingered his nose and grinned. "This'll be one time being a lush comes in handy. I know practically every bartender from Sunset and Vine to out here—and others, too. Sure, they'll remember us. Who could forget Virginia?" He nodded toward the pleasant, tinkling sounds from the kitchenette. . . . "She's an A-production in 3-D and color."

Pete nodded. "Okay so far. When did you get here?"

Dan shut his eyes and mumbled to himself. "Première . . . that started at nine-thirty. Musta been over about eleven."

"Eleven ten."

"Okay. . . . Eleven ten. . . . We skipped early to avoid the mob. . . . Besides, nobody was going to ask for my autograph. We hit the first bar at eleven. One quick one. I think it was Spigotti's place. Yeah, it was, because I told Carlo about the première and the party at Derwent's. We stopped for another quick one at . . . I'll remember it later. I guess it was twelve when we got here."

"Must have been earlier. Katon called me at twelve-thirty and said the case was solved, so the police must have . . ."

"So it was quarter to twelve. . . . Say, what are you? A District Attorney?"

Pete sighed. "Loeb Films is too mixed up in this. I've got to know what to release to the papers. And just when I'm starting a campaign on a new star!"

"A new star? Who're you beating the drums for now? Somebody I know? Emery? He deserves it. . . . Or Corliss? She's pretty old to build into . . ."

"I don't even know her myself. This is Jake's private dream and I've got to saddle his nightmare. . . . But get back to your story. You got here . . . it must have been before twelve. Even Fels doesn't solve cases in half an hour. Give him at least forty minutes."

"I'll give him forty-five. Say we got here at quarter of twelve. . . . Only Fels didn't solve it. Germaine handed it to him on a platter. Anyway, we got here and piled out. The lights were on at Derwent's and the door was open. I looked in—and saw him."

Pete waited for the actor to go on. Finally he prodded him with: "Well, what then? Did you go in?"

"No! That room even smelled dead. I came over here and phoned the police—and we've been cooped up here ever since, practically. Fels took us all over a little while ago to look at the scene and have Germaine re-enact her part. Is she a ham! She looked like Grable discovering a cockroach in her teacup."

"Did you talk to any reporters? Did they get any shots?"

"Fels wouldn't let us—or them. Say!" Dan bawled in the direction of the kitchenette. . . . "What's taking so long with those drinks?" He explained to Pete, "She's making what she calls a Kennesaw Kick and it's a secret . . . like the atom bomb."

"Then what happened?" Pete prodded.

"We came back here to our drinks . . . and let's hope the new batch lives up to Virginia's promise. . . . Hey, Virginia!"

A thin giggle answered him, and then a girl called, "I was just samplin' one, honey. They're just like home." And then she came to the door. She was tall and coolly beautiful in the impersonally beautiful manner of a superior store window dummy, and very, very blonde. She stood in the doorway, a tall glass in her hand, as if she were used to posing in doorways. Pete suspected she was a photographer's model.

Dan nodded toward her. "That's Virginia. She's from Tennessee."

Virginia smiled very slowly, as if a director had told her to smile, and looked at Pete. "I like my men long and loose-jointed. . . ." She took one long drink, eyeing him over the rim of the glass, and fell flat on her face. She lay there, breathing heavily, her drink making a dark stain on the rug.

Sally giggled, and Carter leaped to his feet, but Dan beat him to the girl's side. He turned her over with a toe under her shoulder and she flopped squishily on her back. Dan stooped and picked her up easily and took her out through another door, glancing over his shoulder at Pete and Bill. . . . "Passed out. Be right back."

"Dump her on the bed by the window, Dan. She'll get some air." Germaine made no effort to follow them and even stopped Carter with a slight gesture. "Leave 'em alone." She took a long swig of her drink and grinned at Carter over the rim of the glass. "Most likely he planned it this way, only he didn't expect it to happen here. Instead, a murder got in the way." She tossed off the last of her drink and started for the kitchenette, Bill lumbering beside her.

Pete stopped her. "Just a sec, Germaine. There's some questions I'd like to ask, so I'll know what to say to the papers. . . ."

"Tell 'em Ed Derwent was askin' for it and he got it. . . ." Her mouth twisted bitterly and one shoulder hunched aggressively. "I just feel sorry for that kid who did it. She'll go through hell—but I guess she's been through that already if she knew Derwent."

Pete hated to ask this question and he dreaded the answer. "Who is she? Anyone from Loeb?"

Germaine turned and eyed him up and down, as if she were investigating for termites. Her voice didn't slide upward angrily; it just whipped out, a low, angry monotone. . . . "You louse. A guy killed . . . some kid that did it eating her heart out, scared crazy . . . and you want to know if Loeb Films is mixed up in it. . . ."

Pete sighed. "Sure, sure. . . . And you have my permission to spend the next three weeks thinking up new names for me. But just the same, I've got a job to do, and that's protect Loeb Films—and your job—and jobs for hundreds of other people. A thing like this can kill a picture company. I can't bring Derwent back, but I can keep him from taking Loeb Films with him." Then, remembering the stack of photographs in Derwent's bedroom, Pete added forlornly, "I hope."

"Okay, Pete. Sorry. . . . I'm a bit jumpy myself tonight." Germaine licked her full, sensuous lips. "I'll tell you what I can."

Bill, who had been looking his bewilderment as to just which side of this argument he would enter, grinned at the amicable settlement.

"Just tell me what you told Fels." Pete watched her closely. "How close did you tie Derwent to Loeb Films?"

"Just that he'd just finished a job there. I knew he had, because I called him myself, through Central Casting."

"Well, look, Germaine, if you saw this kid kill Derwent, why didn't you report it right away? Scared?" He glanced at Bill. "Or is this cop making you tongue-tied?"

Germaine turned to study the towering bulk of Bill Katon and smiled at him. He wriggled like an amiable bear, and Germaine chuckled. Pete felt it was perhaps the first easy thing she'd done all evening. Even her mouth looked more rested when she swung back to Pete. "You think I'm scared of him? He's my man. Aren't you?" And Germaine eyed the big ex-Marine frankly. "By the way, what's your name?"

"It's Katon, Bill Katon," Pete supplied for her, since Bill didn't seem capable of remembering it at the moment.

"Let me get a drink. I'm as dry as Death Valley. . . ." Germaine stepped into the kitchen and came out holding a drink that looked mild and colorless. "Virgina's Special." She raised the glass to her lips.

"Now, why didn't you tell the police about the murder when you first saw it?"

Germaine lowered the glass in exasperation. "I've been over that fifty times with Fels. I didn't know it was murder. All I saw then was this girl, sneaking out of Derwent's with a gun in one hand and a big black purse. . . ."

"And the girl? Anybody from Loeb?"

"You and Loeb. No. It was Derwent's new sweetie. I don't know where he picked her up, but she's been around a lot recently. I've seen 'em here—and at night clubs."

Pete sighed wearily. "Who the devil is she?"

Germaine shut her mouth tightly and then sighed. "I don't know."

"Then how did you identify her for Fels?"

"The picture. I identified her picture. Derwent had . . ."

"I've seen some samples."

"Not that kind. This kind even a Baptist preacher wouldn't mind showing his narrow-minded mother. She might as well have left her calling card. And now do you mind? If I don't take this drink, I'll die."

A hand reached around Pete and slapped the drink from her hand.

"If you do you will die."

Germaine stared down at her empty hand, her spattered dress and another stain on the rug. "Dan, that was a crazy kind of joke."

Pete pivoted and stared at the taut, twitching muscles of Dan Kelley's lean, expressive face.

"One of them just killed Virginia. . . ." And suddenly Hollywood's tough guy was beating his fist slowly against Pete's arm, crying in great, choking sobs that shook his massive shoulders and knotted the heavy cords in his throat.

# 5

Pete skirted the dampness on the rug and strode over to the young actor, his legs feeling strangely stiff and light.

"How'd you know the drink was poisoned?"

Kelley's hand beat twice more and then stopped, his ugly, ravaged face twisted up. A muscle twitched along his jaw. "It was cyanosis. Couldn't have been anything else. Cyanide works quick."

"You recognized it?"

Dan nodded. "Obvious. Typical reaction. Soon as I got her on the bed I recognized it—too late. Stricture of the columnar muscles, collapse of the pulmonary system, irregular cardiac disturbance, typical blue cyanosis of lips, and rapid, post-mortem flush."

"You sound like a doctor."

"I was." Kelley grinned crookedly, "At least a medical student. . . . But I couldn't stand the sight of blood." He laughed mirthlessly—at filmland's tough young mug unable to stand the sight of blood. Then he wiped a hand roughly across his face, as if he were angry with it. "And anyway, who would trust a doctor who looks like a gangster?" He thrust his angry, contorted face up at Pete. "Would you want that face bending over your sickbed?"

"No, I wouldn't, Dan." But he said it softly, his hand on the actor's shoulder, easing him back in the chair. "So you spotted it as poison."

"Too late. Only it is always too late with cyanide. I thought she'd passed out and I wasn't paying too much attention." His hand caught Pete's sleeve and he pulled him close. "Who'd want to kill her? She was a nice kid."

Peter eased Dan's hand from his sleeve. "It wasn't meant for Virginia. I think it was meant for Germaine."

Pete heard a gasp behind him and whirled. Germaine, half crouched to speak to Dan, slowly straightened. "Me? I need a drink." She turned.

Bill Katon's big, square body blocking the kitchenette door reminded her, and she shivered. "I don't think I'll ever be able to drink again," She frowned at Pete. "Why me?" Her eyes swiveled away from his, canting wildly around the room, as if she could pick out the murderer among those stricken faces.

"Maybe it wasn't, but this is your house. It was your liquor," Pete pointed out, and then added, with sudden conviction, "and you were a witness at a murder—the only one who could identify the murderer."

Germaine shut her eyes and swayed.

Pete picked up the phone. He glanced around. "Anybody know Derwent's number? Fels and his gang are there," he added in explanation. Germaine gave him a number and he dialed. A moment later he heard a guarded voice saying "Yes." And then, faintly, he could hear the aside: "Chief, it's another one," which Pete suspected referred to an earlier phone call.

"Tell Fels there's been a murder—at Germaine Winters'."

The voice was startlingly clear, as if a masking hand had been jerked from the mouthpiece. "It *is* another one."

Now it was out of his hands. Pete hung up and turned to the five in the room. His eyes ignored Bill, massive and still, guarding the kitchenette. "You might start remembering now which of you has been in that room." The startled glances that flashed between Sally, Germaine and Carter Brainerd told him none of them had thought of that.

Germaine reached out vaguely for a chair and sat. Fortunately there was one behind her, for her hand missed it entirely and Pete was sure her legs wouldn't have held her another minute. She touched one hand to her hair and then looked at it stupidly, as if she couldn't remember having seen it before. She spoke more to the newly strange hand than to Pete. "You mean one of them might have. . . ." Her voice trailed off and she dropped her hand.

Dan Kelley glared up from his furious dark brooding at the damp stain on the rug. "Good Lord, Pete. Not one of us."

"Bynum Fels is going to want to know about all of you. And for that matter—you too, Germaine. After all, you *didn't* take that drink—and you *didn't* die. Virginia did. You could have planned it that way." As Germaine's head started wagging a slow, puzzled denial, Pete shrugged. "Fels can figure it like that. I don't think he will."

Fels didn't. In fact, on the way over he seemed to have come to the conclusion that his witness had been murdered right under his thin, aristocratic nose—and even Germaine's obvious aliveness didn't shake him from that conviction for the first few minutes of his whirlwind occupation of the bungalow. In fact, when he finally got the victim's identity straightened out he seemed slightly irritated with Germaine—and then, quite suddenly, vastly relieved. He grinned with bleak cheerfulness. "So the murderer slipped up." He stood there tapping his foot with such smug assurance that Pete was sure Fels was congratulating himself inwardly for having, in some obscure way, tripped up the murderer. "I've still got my star witness."

"It was the bacardi. . . ." A noncommittal voice spoke from the doorway of the kitchenette, and a hand held a bottle aloft, carefully wrapped in what looked like a whimsically decorated dish towel.

Germaine pointed at the bottle. "That's my . . . nobody ever touches . . . Oh!" She went pale and caught at Bill's arm, burying her face against his shoulder. Pete watched Bill's face redden almost to apoplexy before he took Germaine's shoulders and turned her around.

Pete shook her lightly. "That's your what that nobody ever touches?"

It took time to get it out of her, but she finally made it clear that she kept the bacardi for herself—for a night-cap so she could sleep. Carter admitted knowing it was Germaine's habit. Sally, after considerable confusion, during which she couldn't seem to remember her name or anything else, confirming Pete's standing opinion that she was Loeb's stupidest starlet, finally managed to recall that she knew about it, too. So did Dan. And Germaine said, with frightened anger, that any of her friends would know it.

"Was this girl you saw at Derwent's—was she a friend? Would she know about it?"

Germaine shook her head. "No, I didn't know her. . . ." Then she gnawed a finger, peering up at Pete. . . . "But Derwent knew—and he knew this girl—and he could have told her."

Fels nodded thoughtfully at this. "Obviously what happened."

He swung around to the policeman, who still held the bacardi bottle gingerly. "Are you sure that's the one that's poisoned?"

The officer nodded. "Smells like almonds. I'm not tasting it. None of the others do." He thought that over for a moment. "And I'm not tasting them, either." But he looked as if he might like to.

"Take everything in there down to the laboratory for tests."

"For cyanide first," Pete offered, and saw Fels turn to look speculatively at him.

"You movie people use a lot of cyanide."

"But not for murder."

Fels smiled nastily, "Don't be too sure. Where do you keep your developing supplies?"

"In the lab, naturally."

Fels chewed on that for a moment. "So any one of these people had access, too. . . ."

"Don't be too sure. You!" He stabbed a slender finger at Dan. "Where's the film lab?"

"Huh?" Kelley looked up from his anguished stupidly, "Lab? How should I know? I'm an actor." He frowned, "Anyway, you have to belong to the union to get in. Or own the joint."

Fels sighed. "Okay. And take that stuff away."

"Hey!" Germaine started a protest and then slumped back in her chair. "Oh, go ahead. Take it all."

"There's another thing, Mister Fels. . . ." A detective thrust his head over the policeman's shoulder. "The screen has been cut out, and there's mud on the windowsill and what looks like a toe-print on the wall outside—like somebody scraped his foot trying to get in."

"A man's footprint?" Fels looked briefly annoyed.

"Can't tell. Just spotted it with my flash. We can take a better look from outside."

Fels nodded. "But make sure you're not messing up footprints when you do. I'll go with you, to make sure."

The detective grumbled something about knowing his work and heaved his way around the policeman with the bottle. Fels and two other men, police cameramen, followed him out. Pete sat down and let his head ache.

Fels came back, scowling, and answered Pete's unspoken question. "Can't tell. Could be a woman's shoe—or a man's. Just a toe mark, and scraped at that. A piece of the screen is cut away—from the outside—and folded back to get at the latch. Somebody came in that way, all right. The mud on the sill is mashed, where the screen was pulled down into it, so it was opened and then closed, after the murderer got out, probably." He glanced around. "Though she probably could have walked right out the door." Fels sat heavily. "I'm going to give somebody what for, letting a murderer wander around loose, right while we're here."

That meant he didn't suspect anyone in the party, and somehow it was a relief. If Marilyn had gone undetected this long, perhaps nobody had seen her except himself.

A cop stuck his head in the front door. "Fels?" And as the assistant D.A. swung around, he coughed. "Thought I might find you here. There's a phone call from TWA. Guy says they're confirming Derwent's reservations to New York. What'll I tell 'em?"

Fels puffed out his cheeks for an angry retort and then switched to suffering patience. He sighed. "Do you think he'll be using it?"

"No sir."

"Then tell 'em so!" The cop jerked his head away and disappeared.

Dan Kelley stared at the open door and then at Fels. "I guess that's what he was talking about."

Fels sighed again. "Who?"

"Derwent. That is what the party was for. He said something about a 'personal appearance'—and sniggered. It didn't make sense, because extras like Derwent don't make personal appearances." He looked at Pete for confirmation and added a mild reservation: "Not usually."

Fels nodded. "So he was going to New York . . . but he won't go now. Maybe he was skipping out on this girl, and she didn't like it." He stood up suddenly and looked down at Pete. "Ready?"

"What for?"

"Formal identification of Derwent. So I can wind up this case."

Pete grinned slowly. "No! I'm going to bed."

Fels blustered. "Now see here, how can I wind up this case by morning if I don't have an official identification?"

"Nuts! Catch your murderer. And tomorrow I'll be down and make an official identification. I'm not holding up a thing, and you know it—except maybe a chance for you to crow that you solved a case in less than twelve hours. Which you didn't. Germaine did it for you. And you'd better protect her."

"I will!" Fels stood up and aimed his finger dramatically. "She's under arrest as a material witness."

Germaine looked up drowsily, said "Boo!" and then yawned. "Can I sleep in jail?"

Fels waved them all away. "I'll notify you about the inquest."

Pete took Dan's arm and turned him away from the long wicker basket that wobbled gruesomely between two white-coated attendants.

He wheeled the car out of the tangle of police cars, waved a good-bye to Katon who was solicitously guiding Germaine to the assistant D.A.'s limousine. He swung into the main street and out toward his home, an apartment kept in order by a Mrs. Hariwisc who regarded Pete as her personal cross and private segment of the bewildering Hollywood zoo. At a brightly lighted corner he stopped and bought a paper but didn't read it until he had gotten Dan home and in bed with two drinks. The Hollywood tough guy fell asleep instantly, looking only young, puzzled, and somewhat sulky.

Pete picked up the paper and turned expertly to the drama page. A picture of the girl at the preview stared out at him, her young face hauntingly lovely, pathetically strained, desperately seeking something. And under it was a caption:

"Jacob Tobias, Head of Loeb Films, says, 'I Want That Girl.'"

Pete folded himself into his own bed and slept until morning, certain that he had at least launched a campaign that would keep Loeb Films in the public eye for some time—possibly as long as a week.

He awoke the next morning before Dan and crawled sleepily after the morning paper, to look for his follow-up. Sometimes they didn't give it. He rattled the paper open and saw the picture again—and the caption—and beside it! Pete blinked and stared.

Beside it was another picture—the same girl but a different pose—a pose of sweet innocence—a picture a Baptist minister wouldn't mind showing his narrow-minded mother. The same girl! There wasn't any mistaking it. It was fiendish. It couldn't happen. But it had. Under the sweet innocence was a mocking caption:

"Bynum Fels, Assistant District Attorney, says, 'I Want That Girl—for Murder.'"

# 6

"Peter Hack!" When Jacob Tobias yelled his name in full—and in that tone of voice—he wanted attention—undivided attention.

He got it. Pete straddled a chair, rested his arms on the back and regarded his boss.

"First, we gotta find the girl. . . ." Jake held up a plump pink finger. "Before Fels gets her. For you is easy." Another finger went up. "Next, we get her story and prove she is innocent—the victim of a conspiracy. A black-hearted conspiracy."

"Wait a minute, Jake. This is life—not a new Tobias script."

"Script! Script! That's it. I get my best writers to turn out a script about how this girl, sweet and innocent, is caught in the web of a black-hearted conspiracy. A fiendishly clever district attorney is hounding this poor girl. Maybe she had spurned him. Or should we make her an heiress but she don't know it? Like in 'Hearts Forsaken'? And when you find her and clear this cloud, we star her in the picture." Jake spread his hands happily on the desk. "Look, I do your work for you . . . the writers' work for them . . . and I don't even ask for screen credit. Now go find her."

Pete lifted his hat with two fingers and used two to scratch his head. He felt baffled, as he nearly always felt baffled after a session with Jake in a creative mood. "Sure, just find the girl. . . with the entire Los Angeles police force looking for her. I'm so glad you're doing my work for me. Now, just where do I look?"

"Details!" Jake was gathering up papers and standing up. "I gotta see Phillips a minute and then I call a story conference. Go see Central Casting—or ask Fels for her address." Jake trundled past him, gathering momentum. He charged through the door and Pete flipped through behind him. The door closed with a bang that showered down a little tinkle of broken glass, and Emily Fishbein, Jake's personal secretary, squealed. Pete followed in Tobias' wake at a dead run, marveling at the little man's fat, twinkling legs and their capacity to take him around corners without caroming off walls. He came to an abrupt stop and whipped open a door marked private and all but slammed it on Pete's nose—almost, but not quite.

Pete couldn't rightly blame Alwyn Phillips for looking startled, but their entrance, though abrupt, was scarcely enough to start the man shaking, and make him drop the heavy, silver-framed picture. The glass shattered, and Phillips looked down at it as if he were going to cry. Jake swooped on, stooped and snatched up the picture. "I get Supplies to put in a new glass." He handed the banker a sheaf of papers. "Reports on the gross of 'Beggars May Ride'—three millions so far. Ain't bad, huh?" And then he looked at the silver-framed photograph. "Hmmm. . . . So much retouching it takes to put a smile on Old Vinegarpuss. . . ."

Phillips reached for the photograph. "I'll thank you not to speak that way of my Aunt Amelia."

Jake tucked the big picture under his arm. "I get it fixed." He flipped the picture out again and looked at it. "I never see a picture of her before, now I think of it.

Nice. They must embalm her in maple syrup first, to get such a smile."

"That is Amelia Alwyn you're speaking of, and she's worth millions, Mr. Tobias." Phillips reached again for the picture, but Tobias forestalled him by tucking it once more under his arms.

"Millions, yes—and not a penny made her happy. Such an unhappy woman. And such a son. Is good maybe he's dead." Jake tapped the papers he had thrust in Phillips' hands. "Reports like that should make you happy. Three millions gross on a picture costs us maybe five hundred thousand."

The mention of such figures riveted Phillips' attention and he stared down at the report, but he still held a lingering remnant of the conversation. "Aunt Amelia won't acknowledge he's dead. A whim. Three million gross. Preposterous. For tripe like that? I saw 'Beggars May Ride'—utterly inconsequential fluff."

"Nothing inconsequential about three million dollars." And Jake whipped around, almost stumbling over Pete. "What! Ain't you found that girl yet? Go on out and find her. Now."

Phillips heard that. "Mister Tobias!" His voice was scandalized. "You're not continuing that preposterous search for the unknown girl! Impossible. Why, she's involved in some murders. You can't drag the studio through any such imbroglios."

"Were already in it. I gotta get us out. Pete is gonna find that girl and prove she didn't commit those murders and we make a star out of her. Simple." Jacob Tobias scuttled out the door and slammed it behind him, leaving Pete alone with a badly befuddled Phillips.

"I don't understand the man. Really I don't, Mister Hack. Any normal person would drop this woman like something unclean." Phillips delicately dusted his hands to show how he would get rid of her. "A woman involved in two murders—wanted by the police. Surely you can persuade him to forget this whole thing and let the law take its course. Why, the man must be insane."

Pete laid a finger on the edge of the stacked reports and flipped through them. "I'd like to be insane—three million dollars worth." He walked out, somehow much less troubled by Jake's crazy assignment.

He was halfway across Loeb Films' huge lot, on the way to his car, when he realized someone was calling him, and calling him in a way that reminded him of hills and sagebrush. He swung around. It was Tom Brady.

"Why didn't you just yell 'Hi-Ho, Silver!' and be done with it?"

The heavy-featured Western star, trotting up on high stilted heels, looked pained. "That's the Lone Ranger, podner. My hoss is named 'Phantom' and I just give a ghostly cry like 'Yooohoooo-oooo, Phaaantum.'" Tom Brady's familiar cry echoed resoundingly down the aisle of buildings. Several people turned to stare and then went on.

Pete started walking on and Brady fell into step beside him, thrusting back his huge white Stetson and mopping a usually placid brow with an enormous bandanna handkerchief.

"Uh, podner, I been readin' about this here murder. Hombre named Derwent."

Brady was as subtle as one of the branding irons he wielded so expertly and Pete knew he was being pumped. It interested him that Brady, the clean-living, high-minded Western star, should be curious about Derwent.

"Yeah. Derwent got killed last night."

"Heard this Derwent was mixed up in things."

Pete started to answer, and then he looked at Brady, startled. Fels had been most particular not to give out anything on Derwent's activities for fear it would damage his eventual case against the girl—so there had been no hint, even, of Derwent's blackmail proclivities in the papers. Yet Brady seemed to be headed in that direction. Pete nodded slowly, waiting for Brady's next line.

"I knew the feller . . . jest casual." Brady was watching for a reaction. "Anybody sorta mention it?"

Pete shook his head. "Nobody mentioned your name." He watched Brady. "But of course I left before they finished going through his files."

Brady groaned. The big Western star was gauntly strained, his bronzed face steaked and puttyish. "Papers. . . . I neva thought o' them." Brady wouldn't. Although Pete didn't subscribe to the local theory that Tom had had to be taught to sign his name, he was sure he would never think of papers.

"Look, Tom, you knew Derwent more than casually—and he had something on you."

Brady's protest was wild. "No! I jest knew him."

"How? Where'd you meet him?"

"I got a cottage . . . sort o' hideaway . . . on the court."

Pete was shocked. Just why, he didn't know, except that he had come to believe that Brady was as forthright and direct as his character in the films. "That place has a reputation, Tom. Not a nice reputation."

"I know now. I didn't when I took it. Hit jest seemed like a nice place I could get away to."

"Get away to? Good Lord, Brady, you've got a thousand acre ranch down the valley."

"That's what I was gettin' away from, Pete. I'm awful tahrd o' my public sometimes. An' I git powerful sick o' kissin' that horse. I jest wanted a place to rest an' smoke tailor-mades." Tears of weariness dimmed Brady's mild blue eyes. "An' git out'n these boots. They cramp my toes."

Pete swallowed a laugh. "And Derwent was blackmailing you for that? How? How much did you give him?"

"Jest give him a leg up with some people—movie people—an' lent him a little money. Mebbe couple o' hundred."

Pete did not laugh then. "Don't worry about Derwent. Or Fels. Nobody's gonna give a hoot if you do relax once in a while, Tom. And certainly Fels isn't going to make anything of it."

"Uh-huh." But Brady still wasn't happy. "On'y that ain't the wust of it."

Pete felt his stomach shiver. More was coming. "A girl?" That sounded more in Derwent's class.

Brady nodded solemnly. "Yeahs ago. I warn't more'n a kid." It was pouring out now, no way to stop the rolling tide. "Down in a cowtown in Texas . . . Crooked Gulch, Texas. I remember hit like hit was yestiddy. Myrtle was a right perty girl, too."

"And she got in trouble?"

Brady's eyes were miserable. "Yup, sure did. And her paw figgered it was me, since I'd been sorta courtin' her . . . and he come after me. Chased me outa the town . . ."

"Well, were you responsible? Did you get the girl in trouble?"

"Me?" Brady looked hurt. "Pete, I wouldn'ta harmed a hair of her sweet head."

"All right, if you weren't to blame, what the devil could Derwent blackmail you for?"

"My public, man." Brady was astonished. "Why, it'd ruin me. Tom Brady run out o' town by an old man." Brady's voice sank. "I wouldn'ta minded so much ef he'd used a six-gun. My public mighta stood for that." Brady's voice dropped and died.

Pete was puzzled. "What made it so awful, Brady?"

"The ole man used a shotgun—a measly, twelve-gauge shotgun."

Pete leaned against the wall they were passing and hooted with laughter.

# 7

Pete went to his apartment to collect Dan, knowing Fels would want to see him.

Dan was brooding by the radio, a long drink that looked suspiciously dark and strong resting on the arm of the chair. It would make rings, but that was Mrs. Hariwisc's worry, not Pete's. "They haven't caught her yet." Dan spoke without looking up from the louvres of the radio loudspeaker, as if by glaring at it he could extract the news a moment sooner.

"They will." Pete motioned to the closet. "Put your coat on. We're going to see Fels. He's probably having kittens now, wondering where you are."

"Let him wonder!" Dan drank deeply from the glass. "That won't bring her back." His permanently angry face twisted up to glare at Pete. "She was a sweet kid. I might have married her. Okay, I'll go." He stood up, a little unsteadily, and started for the closet.

The air braced Dan back to sobriety but didn't improve his disposition. Neither did the lounging reporters around Fels' office door, as he and Pete shoved their way through.

Pete went on into Fels' office when Bill Katon stood in the doorway beckoning. Fels was scowling portentously into one of a stack of little black books that Pete suspected had come from Derwent's cottage. And the idea gave him momentary worms in the stomach.

"I came down to identify Derwent for you—officially."

"It's been done." Fels waved him into a chair with the little black book. "Hammond came down this morning. Glad somebody can be co-operative."

"I'm co-operative. Just don't get me riled."

Fels smiled bleakly. "You rile easy."

"And I'm not saying anything about the way an assistant D.A. grabs himself a lot of publicity using my story for a lead."

Fels leaned back in his chair and held the little black book between his hands as if it were a hymnal. "That wasn't publicity for me—but it made a very excellent tie-in to get the girl. If one picture is good—two is more than twice as good. Everybody will notice *both* pictures now—and I'll get my killer."

"And if she isn't the killer?"

"Then she can tell her story. I don't have to believe it."

"I've got a hunch you'll believe it."

Fels sat forward suddenly, slapping the book on his desk. "Look, Hack, I'm not fooling in this case. You may not like me, and it's for sure that I don't like you. You're too flip. But murder is something you can't be flip with. I've seen those stories you gave out last night—about the mystery girl at the première. And frankly, they stink. Very cheap publicity."

"From where I sit, it begins to look like very expensive publicity."

"You know what I mean. The girl is a stooge, a plant. You've got her under wraps, and last night you sprung her. Only she committed a murder first. Now I want her. Bring her in."

"Good grief, Fels." Pete launched into the story of Jacob Tobias and his aberration. "And honestly, I really don't know the girl. I'm trying as hard as you are to find her. I thought my picture would bring her in. What gal wouldn't come screaming to the gates—if she thought there was a picture contract waiting for her? Now she'll never come forward—not after you added your tail to the kite." He smiled wryly. "For once I think you overreached yourself, Fels. It was good publicity but damn poor judgment."

Fels slumped sulkily in his chair. "It wasn't publicity. I want that girl. Somebody is going to spot those pictures and turn her in."

"She'd have come in—with just my bait out. Your stuff will scare her off. And you can bet your next month's pay she's gone into deep hiding. Incidentally, how much is next month's pay?"

"It's . . ." Fels shut his mouth angrily. "None of your business." He shook the black book at Pete. "You aggravate me." He stopped glaring at Pete and looked at the book again, slowing its emphatic waggle. "Oh." He reversed the book and opened it. "Let's see if you're co-operative. This seems to be Edgar Derwent's address book. Girls. Some of them I can eliminate, because I know them—and I know those aren't our unknown."

"You played around in Derwent's set?"

"I mean," Fels almost screamed, "I know who they are through Central Casting, and other ways we have of checking."

Pete reached for the book before Fels burst a blood vessel. "I'll do my best, Fels. And I mean it." He thumbed through the book, noting Fels' red pencil checks. Those he could eliminate. He ran his finger down a page. "Check off Gladys Jordan. She died of pneumonia last March."

"So that's why Central Casting didn't have her listed."

"And Alice Chambers. I've seen her around. Can't remember where. But she's not your unknown. And Vyvyan Del Ruth." Pete went on scanning the pages.

"Why?"

Pete looked up. "Vyvyan Del Ruth is just too phony. Anybody with that name is bound to be a Hollywood career girl. And our unknown isn't a career girl."

"We'll skip her for the moment. Any others?"

"Strike off Consuelo Fernandez."

"You know her?"

Pete looked up, annoyed. "Look, Fels, anybody with that name would have to be Spanish, if it's real, or look Spanish, if it's phony. Your unknown isn't the Spanish type at all . . . just nice, wholesome American." Good Lord, if he kept this up, he would talk himself into liking the girl.

"I see what you mean—about the Spanish type." Fels sat back and nodded agreement with own inner thoughts. "You know, Hack, you're very intelligent, in many ways. You'd make a first-rate detective."

"When they start paying first-rate detectives a thousand a week, I'll take the job." He handed the book back to Fels. "You can check off Lois Acton. She's a waitress in the diner across from Loeb's. And the one that just says 'Agnes.' She's a B girl at Carlo Spigotti's place. I recognize her phone number, and I think I remember 'Agnes,' a blonde who never recovered from an attack of Jean Harlowe."

Fels accepted the book, tapping it on the edge of his desk. "Spigotti, huh? That racketeer! I'd like to pin something . . ." His eyes came back to Pete. "I think I know the girl—and she isn't the one. Thanks, Hack. You've been considerably more co-operative than I expected. And you can't blame me for using your own tricks, can you?" The dapper assistant D.A. stood up, his thin mouth in what he no doubt thought was an ingratiating smile.

"Not at all." Pete didn't, somehow, see the extended hand. "I don't blame you. In fact, I think I might even take a leaf out of your book." And Pete smiled at that.

But Fels was pleased. He forgot the unshaken hand and used it to nurse his mustache. "Well, all of us can learn."

Pete nodded to Bill Katon's amiable bull-dozer face, winked and went on through the outer office, where Dan was in the first stages of being comforted by a blonde secretary.

Outside, in the car, he chuckled. A leaf from Fels' book. That wasn't bad. Of course, it wasn't literally a leaf, but four of those addresses stuck in Pete's mind. Four names and addresses that didn't fit any of the familiar patterns of Hollywood. And while Fels was checking all the other unknowns, Pete was going after those four.

He started the car.

# 8

He didn't beat Fels' man to the first one. He saw one of the district attorney's detectives turning away from the door as he drove up. There was no triumph there—just the stolid, determined set of broad shoulders as the man slid himself into the police car. So the first girl was out. Pete took out his hastily scribbled list and checked off Belle Sturgess. Fels was thorough. His men would go through Derwent's book steadily, one by one, skipping only the known entrants. Pete would have to be content with short cuts, and hope they worked.

The next was a dud—in more ways than one. The Annie Dawson of Derwent's notebook with thin, drab and inclined to be whiny, peering at him around the edge of the door with eyes mildly distended by what Pete suspected was goiter. "There must be some mistake, mister. I didn't order a vacuum cleaner!"

"But you are Annie Dawson, aren't you?"

"Yes, and I've got a vacuum cleaner." The door shut hurriedly, as if the woman were afraid he might try to collect money.

Pete went back to the car and looked up the next address. Janet West. He started off, wondering if the vacuum cleaner gag would work again. All he needed was a glimpse of the girl—and he'd know. Maybe he'd better make this next one nylons. Fels' men might get curious if there were too many vacuum cleaner salesmen just ahead of them at each suspect's place.

Janet West evidently lived in a boarding house, because a sign in the glass paneled door said emphatically, "No Vacancies!" Pete rang the bell and waited patiently on the gritty porch. It wasn't exactly a first-class boarding house, either. And the neighborhood had something of a reputation—a slightly smelly reputation. And the boarding house was slightly smelly, too. Pete got a whiff of it as the door opened and a thin, angular woman, bunchily dressed under a cover-all apron, stood guard inside. She pointed a bony finger at the sign, "No vacancies," and started to close the door.

"Is Janet West in?"

The door jittered uncertainly for a moment and the woman glared. "That she ain't. Not any more. And that's what comes of taking in just anybody because your heart's in the right place. I don't see why I ever come here from Ioway in the first place. All this talk about sunshine and carefree living. Hmmmph! Lot of it I've seen, slaving away here like a—a slave. And then people run up board bills on you. And I treated her nice as you please, like my own daughter, if I had one, and not one cent, even when I give her a week to get it up in . . ."

Pete straightened out the monologue well enough to realize that Janet West had left, either on her own or by request, and that a board bill was unpaid. He got out his wallet, which the woman eyed suspiciously. He let her see the sheaf of bills and then drew out a print from the newsreel shot.

"I'm trying to find my cousin. Her mother asked my mother to ask me to look her up." That ought to sound homey and complicated enough to suit the woman who came from Ioway for a bit of sunshine and carefree living but hadn't found it. The woman nodded appreciatively, her eyes swaying between the wallet and Pete's convertible at the curb. "She sometimes used the name Janet West, and I thought . . ." Pete held up the print. The woman nodded at the photograph. The mystery girl was Janet West!

"That's her. Left here owing a week's room and board. Eight . . . twenty-five dollars." The woman's eyes glazed slightly as he pulled out the bills. . . . She wet her lips. "And storage for her things." The woman computed hastily. "Five dollars."

In one minute the mystery girl found . . . and lost. But thirty dollars had cemented friendship with Mrs. Gorman—Mrs. Alfred Gorman, of Waterloo, Ioway, and Pete went into the slightly fetid air of the parlor.

"Where did she go? Where did she move to?"

Well, she simply didn't know where the girl had gone. Just walked off like that. Said she'd get the money from one of her rich friends and just gone. When? Yesterday at noon.

"And you've already rented her room?"

Mrs. Gorman bridled. "I knew she wouldn't come back. And the way people beg for rooms, you just can't turn 'em down. And I was right: she didn't come back." Mrs. Gorman simpered, "Only, of course, now that you've paid the rent, you'll want her things."

Even while he felt sick inside, Pete remembered to be the indignant relative. "Naturally. . . ." There might be clues there. Store labels, letters, even a diary. He could hope for lots of things. And he wanted to get them quickly and get out, before Fels' men came by.

He couldn't. Mrs. Gorman demanded he check through them first, primly insisting she didn't want it said later she hadn't returned every scrap. So he opened the two brightly new, over-sized fabric cases on Mrs. Gorman's rose-back sofa and stood looking down into them.

They were neatly packed, a soft gray-green wool dress folded lengthwise across the top, its square, semi-tailored collar caught with pert bows at the corners, and two breast pockets flaring in impudent little ears. Pete tried dressing his recollection of her in that, and found he liked it. But that wasn't what he was after. He thrust his hand into the long pocket shirred across the top of the suitcase. Books. He pulled out two, a battered school edition of "Hamlet" and a paper-back copy of Samuel French's "Monologues for Women." He smiled grimly, thinking Mrs. Gorman would never need that particular set of instructions. An envelope slid out and Pete grabbed it. It was a bill from a hat shop in McQueeney, Texas—for $25.00. He whistled softly. Hats came high, even in Texas. Or maybe Janet West had splurged for her trip to Hollywood. He looked at the envelope. It was addressed to *"Miss Janet West, 1927 Sitroux Street, McQueeney, Texas."* And it was postmarked less than a month before. So three weeks ago Miss Janet West had been in McQueeney, Texas—reading "Hamlet" and "Monologues for Women."

He put the bill and books aside and dived again. This yielded a plastic case for toothbrush, paste, and wash rag. Hadn't she even taken her toothbrush? Then she'd meant to come back. Only somewhere along the line a murder had intervened.

He was sure of that now. Her name in Derwent's book, her picture in his files (even without Germaine's story), tied her somehow to the murder. And the première—he mustn't forget that. Janet West had come in terror to the première—within half an hour of the time Edgar Derwent was murdered—and been photographed. Maybe that newsreel shot could be an alibi. He knew it couldn't be. There was at least a half-hour lapse, if Germaine's story could be believed. The M.E.'s findings probably corroborated it or Fels would have mentioned any discrepancy.

The suitcases confused him. Certainly they didn't yield any tangible clues—letters or diaries—but on the other hand they didn't give him the picture of a girl who would have been at Derwent's place at night, or who would have even known the Derwent type. He couldn't place just what it was that gave him that picture, either. It wasn't just the simple dresses, because there were two frivolous evening gowns with very brief, very stilted evening slippers to match. And there was nothing old-maidish about the brevity and sheerness of the underthings. No, it was something else. Something missing. That was it! There weren't any elaborate bottles and jars of cosmetics and perfume. He swung on Mrs. Gorman, interrupting another flood of reminiscences. "Her cosmetics. You know. Crystal jars. Bottles. Stuff like that."

Mrs. Gorman looked scornful. "You certainly don't know your cousin very well. She never used 'em. Just cologne. Oh, she had a lipstick—in her purse. And don't think I'm trying to keep anything back. Them's all her things. Every single, solitary scrap."

"Yes, yes, I'm sure it is. I just thought she had some . . ." Pete muttered vaguely, cramming the suitcases shut. Through Mrs. Gorman's stiff and grayish lace curtains he had seen the police car drive up. If he walked hurriedly out, like a departing guest, maybe they wouldn't recognize him, wouldn't stop him.

They didn't, but Mrs. Gorman's suety wits did. "And we'll just list everything and you can sign it. . . ."

"No need." Pete was getting frantic. "Just a claim will do." He tried to get the idea across to Mrs. Gorman, to get past her thin, stubborn face to what wits she had. "A general release. Just say, 'I relieve you of all responsibility,' and I'll sign it."

Mrs. Gorman muttered that over to herself and shuffled to a monstrous highboy that apparently also converted into a desk. She fumbled under her coverall apron for a jangling bunch of keys and peered nearsightedly at them, selecting with care. "Taking boarders the way I do, I gotta keep things locked up. People are so nosy. You have no idea."

Pete tried edging the two heavy suitcases toward the door—and then knew he was too late. The bell clanged violently somewhere in the back of the house, and Mrs. Gorman groaned. "Can't they read the sign? I got no vacancies. And I got no time to run to the door to tell people I ain't." Mrs. Gorman didn't run, but she got to the door and opened it.

Pete heard the murmur of voices and then Mrs. Gorman's excited yip: "My, my!"—and Bynum Fels' personal stooge brushed past her and into the parlor, grinning sadistically.

"Mister Peter Hack! Ain't the D.A. gonna be happy to see you here. And confiscating evidence! Where's the phone?"

Mrs. Gorman stood in the doorway, hands spraddled on her thin cheeks, eyes wide and vacant. "My, my! Murder!"

Russell, the detective, backed into a straight chair by the phone and sat down, grinning. He didn't even look down as he dialed headquarters. He held the phone in one beefy hand and rubbed his ear with it. Suddenly he stopped rubbing. "Get me Fels . . . Bynum Fels. . . ." He chuckled as Pete flung himself on the rose-back sofa. "This I'm gonna enjoy."

He was still enjoying it an hour later, his heavy frame tilted back in a chair beside the door of one of Mrs. Gorman's 'guest rooms,' his heavy jowls chomping rhythmically on a dead cigar, while Pete lay stretched out on a bed thinly disguised as a studio couch. He was still grinning when Bynum Fels came in from questioning Mrs. Gorman. He was wiping his elegant forehead with a once elegant handkerchief. Fels was unhappy—unhappy and baffled and swearing.

"Where the blazes is Waterloo, Iowa?"

Russell thumped his chair to the floor and stood. "I'll look it up for yuh, chief."

"And blow the place off the map, will you?" He glared at Pete. "And as far as I'm concerned, you can blow too."

Pete stood up. "I thought you'd see it that way."

As he walked down the hall, Mrs. Gorman was beckoning frantically and surreptitiously from the narrow crack of a doorway opposite. Pete stepped sideways, opened the door, slid in and closed it behind him, listening to Bynum Fels' spirited charge down the hallway and his fine, strangled bellow, before Pete turned to face an angry and excited Mrs. Gorman.

Pete had to listen to Mrs. Gorman's plaints against a police department that treated her as no lady in Waterloo, Iowa, had ever been treated. And when that policeman, or whatever, implied that she was running a "house"—the quotes were in Mrs. Gorman's indignant voice—she had no intention of telling him anything. Not a single solitary thing. But Mister Hack was obviously a gentleman who paid his debts and no doubt gave something on account.

With that hint, Pete dragged out his wallet and mentally added another fifty dollars to his expense voucher. He leafed through the bills, pulling off tens slowly while he watched Mrs. Gorman's prominent eyes until they batted appreciatively. He had underestimated Mrs. Gorman by thirty dollars. She folded the bills with practiced rapidity and her hands dived under the cover-all apron, where they did mysterious things in the region of her chest. Only when the hands were in sight again, and smoothing out some of the more conspicuous wrinkles in opposite sleeves, did she speak. She leaned toward him portentously and whispered:

"Dave's Drive-In."

Mrs. Gorman's husky, conspiratorial voice suggested a speakeasy, and Pete almost asked, "Do I say Sweeney sent me?" when he recognized the name as a newly popular all-night hotdog stand out on Sunset Boulevard.

"She works there." Mrs. Gorman said it with all the smug assurance that she might have used to proclaim Janet West a fallen woman.

So far as Pete knew, the only objection to the place was that the girls wore unusually brief costumes. Within five minutes he intended to find out exactly how brief those costumes were—and if Janet West inhabited one of them.

# 9

Fels had finally taken himself, Russell, and the "evidence" off, and Pete sneaked out of Mrs. Gorman's boarding house, wishing he had time for a bath and something to get rid of the stale smell. Bill Katon sat on the curbstone looking like a fire hydrant trying to look human. He looked up at Pete and then at the convertible. "I'm supposed to tail you," he stated dolefully, and then brightened. "But I got an idea that jalopy of yours could lose me in traffic."

"Such a thought scandalizes me. I'd like Mister Fels to have a complete and detailed report on how the other half lives." Pete climbed into the car over the cutaway door.

"Or you could sock me on the jaw and knock me out. You owe me one for that night in Algiers." Bill stood up and thrust out his chin, a broad and not too well shaved target.

"It was in Marrakech . . . and you were drunk."

"Blind drunk," Bill amended happily. "And anyway I can't say Marrakech." He thought that over. "Anyhow, not without getting thirsty."

Pete settled behind the wheel. "If you get caught by a red light, I'll wait for you."

"You mean you want I should tail you?"

"After you've said 'Marrakech' you get thirsty. They serve beer at Dave's Drive-In." Pete started the motor.

"Even the thorn in Mister Fels' flesh must eat." He drove off, watching in the rear-view mirror as Bill lumbered to the police car and swung out behind him.

Dave's Drive-In was garish with neon, even this early, but the paved space around it was almost deserted, so that Pete had his pick of several more or less pleasing damsels in bright and brief attire. He got one and ordered. "The extra-special burger, coffee, deep-dish apple pie . . . and Janet West." He handed her a bill and she took it, tucking it under the tray before she grinned saucily at him.

"Dave don't let his girls date. And anyway, she don't work here any more."

"Oh?" Pete had expected that. "Why?"

"She wouldn't date."

"Oh, like that?"

The girl grinned again and shook her head. "It was too good a line to waste. It ain't like that. But I hear a customer put a bug in Dave's ear about her—and I can think what I want, can't I?"

"You knew her pretty well?"

"Fair. She was only here a few days. Patsy was her pal."

"Could I talk to Patsy?"

"Sure." She started off and turned back. "But the order goes on my check." She went on.

A girl came up on his blind side and clattered a tray against the door. Pete swung around, startled, to face a round, slightly pugnacious face framed in black bobbed hair. Her voice was pugnacious, too. "Okay, talk. I'm Patsy."

The girl was plump. Little rolls of fat bulged over the top of the brief blue patent leather skirt-and-panties, and around the tight, frilled bra. Pete looked at her thoughtfully. "You're spoiling for a fight, aren't you?" He grinned.

The girl didn't answer his grin. "Dolores said you ast for me."

"I bet her name used to be Maggie."

A little of Patsy's belligerence died. "Annie—Annie Callahan. But Dolores sounds better when you're trying to get in the movies."

Pete glanced over his shoulder at the thin, alert girl weaving toward them with a tray. "She trying to get in the movies?"

Patsy shrugged. "Who isn't—in Hollywood? Except me."

Pete pivoted back and grinned at her. "Good. Then I won't have to use that line."

"Like you did on Janet?"

"Hey!" Pete sat up. "What is this? You come over here ready for a fight, your sleeves rolled up."

"We don't wear sleeves—or anything else much. All right, say what you gotta say, an beat it, Mister Derwent. You've done enough damage already, ain't you?"

Pete had to wrestle with his order on the other door of the car and pay his bill before he could turn back to Patsy. "Derwent?" He'd have to go carefully. And time was precious. Any minute Fels' men might somehow learn of Janet's connection with Dave's Drive-In. "Do I look like that guy?"

"How would I know? I never seen you before . . . or Derwent."

Pete dug down for his wallet and held out his celluloid-covered credentials. "Peter Hack, with Loeb Films . . . and I'm looking for Janet West. My boss wants her for a screen test."

Patsy studied the credentials and then Pete's face. She handed him back the wallet. She still hadn't thawed. "That was Derwent's racket?"

"Didn't you see the early morning papers?" He was afraid to mention the noon edition.

"Sure. I read my paper while the butler serves breakfast. All us working girls do. So what?"

"The power of the press. Just that my boss has launched a campaign that'll probably cost him half a million—to find Janet West." He thought of the newsreel print and produced it. "That got in every paper in the U.S. this morning."

Patsy turned for a better light and held up the glossy print. She turned back, grinning. "You mean the kid gets a break? Say, wait'll I tell her. . . ."

This was good! Too good! And Pete had to stop her. His hand grabbed her arm. "Wait. There's a joker."

Patsy swiveled back, her eyes suddenly angry. "I thought there would be."

"It's not that. Look, Derwent's dead—murdered—and Janet's the prime suspect." Patsy gasped but she took it.

"I been wondering. The kid's been in a panic since last night." And then her eyes hardened. "Or are you a cop?"

"I'm just what I told you. And I've got to keep Janet away from the cops—at least until this mess is cleared up."

"So far, I'm doing that job all right . . . and I didn't know the cops wanted her. What's the pitch? Give it quick."

"My boss has slung his neck in a noose—and flung in half a million and is willing to fling more."

"To heck with your boss and the money. I'm thinking of Janet."

"You know where she is."

The girl's eyes were suddenly wary. "I might be able to get in touch with her."

"Well, if the cops ask, you might not, see. I've got to protect her—and I've got the money to do it."

Patsy scowled under dark bangs. "I think you're okay . . . but I'd like to think you over a little while. I'm off at six-thirty. Know where the Blue Raven is?"

"I can find it."

"Be there at seven . . . and you'd better give me a lush order so old Custard Face won't wonder about me bein' out here so long."

Pete opened the wallet. "Make it a dozen hamburgers and six pints of beer. And take 'em to that cop in the prowl car."

"Will he eat 'em?" And as Pete nodded the girl whistled. "This I gotta see."

"How'll we take care of Dolores—in case the cops do turn up? And they will. It's better if they don't know I was asking for Janet." He held the open wallet out to the plump girl.

Patsy took two tens and a five and grinned at him. "And if you want to seal her lips, give her a gate pass."

"I'll do better." Pete whipped out a card and wrote on it. "That'll get her an interview with the casting director, who is only slightly harder to approach than God. You only have to die to meet Him."

Patsy thrust the money and card into the already tight waistband of the skirt.

Pete drove past Bill slowly enough to give the big detective time to pay his bill and follow. They rolled up to the studio gates and in together when Pete signaled the doorman to clear Bill's prowl car. It was funny—having to clear the way for your police shadow.

They stopped near the executive offices and Pete walked over to the police car. Bill's eyes were pleasantly glazed. He burped. "Those hamburgers were swell. Thanks, Pete."

"You ate 'em all? A dozen?" He'd thought of it as a gag.

"I couldn't manage but eight of 'em . . . not after the first six I ordered." He smiled. "But I didn't waste 'em. I brought these four along for a snack. In case I got hungry." He patted a brown paper bag. "I'll wait till you come out." Bill settled deep in the seat, hat over his eyes.

In the upper hall Pete met a surge of people coming out of Jake's private projection room—among them Fels, who was fingering his mustache and looking down at Tobias, continuing a conversation.

"You really think so? I've never thought of the screen as a career, though I see your point. To a certain extent, every trial attorney *is* an actor. You have to have that flair. . . ." Fels even nodded pleasantly to Pete. "And thank you for letting me see those newsreel shots. Not that I can agree with your contention that the girl is innocent. Terrified, yes, but hardly innocent. And that handbag she flung around. It looked heavy. As if it might contain a gun." Fels scowled dramatically. "I wish you'd got what she was saying on the sound track."

"I can tell you. I've watched it often enough," Pete volunteered.

Fels stopped abruptly. "You can tell? Read lips?"

"When you've helped film editors match a sound track to lip movements as much as I have . . ." Pete left that unfinished. "She was yelling, 'Hammy! Hammy! Hammy!' and personally, I think it was unjust criticism, especially as she hadn't even seen Abbott acting yet." That was a dig at the sulky leading man trailing the party.

Abbott looked up, annoyed. "That wasn't funny."

Fels stared at Pete in surprise. "I believe you're right. 'Hammy'—that's just what she was saying. However, I'd like to see it over once again, just to check my impression." Now it was Fels' impression and no longer Pete's.

Tobias heaved a small sigh and turned around, but just at that moment Emily Fishbein stalked out on them. She held a pink slip in her hand. "A message for Mister Fels."

The assistant district attorney started forward and Emily fixed her cold troutish eyes on him. "Your office reports they have located Janet West."

Pete's heart lurched and he felt sick. He hadn't covered well enough.

# 10

Fels stared at the pink slip blankly and repeated, "Located Janet West?" He scowled and then tried to snatch the slip. "Where? Give me that . . ."

Emily adroitly avoided his outstretched hand and rebuked him. "All messages are kept for the files." And then she consented to look down at the slip. "It says you're to report at a place called Dave's Drive-In."

Fels and his three cohorts were off down the hall, to the assistant D.A.'s excited yapping of "Dave's Drive-In . . . Dave's Drive-In!" And Pete felt better. If they hadn't traced her any further than the hamburger stand, she was reasonably safe. Somehow he felt confident of the loyalty and ingenuity behind Patsy's round Irish face.

Pete started down the hall and found Abbott tagging along. The magnificent hunk of ham was still sulking. "It's a good thing you're dropping this girl. Now is the time to build me up. Put a little publicity behind me, and I'll be up there with Gable, Cooper, and Stewart. . . ."

"They can act."

Abbott's handsome profile was marred by a protruding lower lip. "You pretend to think I can't act. But I've got a public . . . an adoring public. Millions. And it wouldn't take much . . ." Abbott was suddenly wheedling. "One good campaign would do it. Like MGM is doing for Burt

Lancaster. A splash like that—not half of what you were going to spend on this screwball idea of Jake's—and you'd have a star. Give me the right vehicle. Something romantic, with fiery undertones, and a fight, a good, brawling fight. Women eat that up—and it builds you up with the men, too. And a couple of good tight love scenes. Ernest Hemingway could write it. Or a part like MacMurray's in 'Double Indemnity.' You could get Frank Gruber to do it."

"In Technicolor?"

"Yes!" Abbott's eyes lighted and his handsome, vapid face turned to Pete before he got the sarcasm. The light died out and Abbott scowled. "You ought to. You ought to do something to draw off this stink Derwent's murder is going to tie on your tail."

"You're wrong, Charlie. Aside from a bad break on the timing of that publicity, there's nothing to tie Derwent's murder to the Loeb Studios. Fels understands that now. You saw it. Jake had him eating out of his hand."

"Yeah." Abbott jerked to a halt and laughed. "And he'll bite it off—when he learns just how thoroughly Derwent is tied to Loeb's tail." He laughed in a weak imitation of a Bogart sneer and turned away abruptly, scuttling down the hall.

Pete looked after him and then turned toward Hammond's office. It might not be a bad idea to check just how closely Derwent was tied to the Loeb studios. Hammond was out—according to what the girl who was substituting for Germaine told him—on Sound Stage Six, checking off the dress extras, normally Germaine's job. The girl looked up Derwent's card, but it gave no clue, except that for the last six months Edgar Derwent had had fairly regular spots in various Loeb productions.

Phillips opened the door and marched in, a sheaf of papers in his hand. "I want," he addressed the room, "a complete report on all social security deductions for the past year."

The girl at the file cabinet looked puzzled and glanced at Pete. Pete didn't bother to look up. "Accounting ought to have 'em. Not Casting." He picked up the phone and called Central Casting. Pete got through to the record clerk and asked how many other studios were using Edgar Derwent—and the answer was baffling—only Loeb. "In fact," the voice went on with damning pleasantness, "it seems that he was originally recommended and placed with us through Loeb Films. You know, we haven't been accepting applications for some . . ." Very softly Pete hung up. Derwent was Loeb's baby.

For once Phillips managed to sense an atmosphere.

"Something wrong?"

Pete nodded. "We're stuck with Derwent, all right. Somebody here recommended him to Central Casting—and nobody else uses him. That makes him very exclusively ours." Pete thumped the table so hard the telephone jangled. "And I'd like to know who!"

Phillips looked distressed. "Isn't there some way you could find out?"

Pete nodded, getting up. "From Germaine Winters—if I could get her out of jail long enough to ask her." He started for the door. "I can try Hammond, but it won't do any good."

"You mean," Phillips was horrified, "Hammond doesn't know what goes on in his own office?"

"Dick Hammond is one of the best casting directors there is. But he's absent-minded. He's even been known to come to work on Sunday." Pete just managed not to slam the door on Phillip's next remark, which would undoubtedly start, "Well, I must say . . ."

Pete knew he'd have to ask Hammond, though undoubtedly the director would not remember. Hammond knew faces, he knew walks, he knew hands, he knew voices—and somewhere, in the magnificent cloud of his mind, he connected them with the right people and got together precisely the right casts— but after the casting was over, he couldn't have told the name of the star, much less an extra. Germaine Winters attended to details.

The sound stage was dark and gloomy, jungle-festooned with ropes and cables and blocked out in odd corners of sets, and stairs that rose to nowhere. Hammond had finished early. Pete started back—and saw a flurry of motion over by the star's dressing rooms. A door squeaked softly and a board creaked. Pete tiptoed toward the sound, suspecting another episode in the minor thievery that troubled all studios.

Then a light stabbed toward him, pinning his shadow, gigantic and distorted, on an enormous blank flat at his side. Pete stepped out of the light, squinting. It came from the window of a dressing room—whose, he couldn't make out in the darkness. A star's dressing room, of course, was like a second home—and like her home, sacred and inviolate and, by the same token, open to her at all times. But there had been something too surreptitious, too furtive and secret about that figure to be a star returning for something forgotten, or for a rest, or even a quiet drink. Pete slid up against the wall and edged his way to the window. He peered cautiously in—and gasped.

Marilyn Courtney, petite and pampered star, was down on her highly publicized knees, industriously sweeping the floor with a small whisk broom!

Pete slid past the window to the door of the dressing room and reached for the knob—and froze. The name, glinting in reflected fight, was certainly not Marilyn Courtney's. Pete had learned to read fairly young. It distinctly said: "Corliss Petry." He flung open the door on a magnificent view of the Courtney derrière.

Marilyn rolled over and sat up in one swift, smooth motion, her lovely elfin face contorted with anger and something like fear. And she was clawing frantically at the grip of a blue-steel automatic thrust in the V of her dress.

"It's caught in the padding." Pete took one long step and leaned down, his thin brown hand closing over Marilyn's wrist. He twisted lightly, heard Marilyn's little squeal of pain, and then with his free hand, very carefully extracted the automatic fending off Marilyn's wild, one-handed blows with his elbow. With the automatic in his hand, he straightened, just in time to avoid a viciously snapping bite at his wrist.

Marilyn wriggled on the floor and came up in one swift, lithe movement, breathing heavily, the corners of her softly perfect mouth sucked in and whitened with rage . . . "You—you." Suddenly she smiled, the tension going out of her, and peered at him from under lowered lashes—one of her more effective poses. "Pete, I'm surprised! I didn't know you went in for being a he-man. . . ." She stepped toward him, her wide eyes twinkling provocatively.

"If Bogart was playing this scene with you, he'd slap you—with the back of his hand." Pete sat down, the automatic lying handily in his lap. "But I'm not Bogart—and I'm not picturesquely tough. I'm just plain, ordinary tough. So sit down there and start talking . . . even if that does sound like a B production script." As Marilyn hesitated he waved the gun. "And I mean it."

"You wouldn't shoot me." But a tiny quaver in her voice made it a question.

"Don't be too sure. It would certainly eliminate a lot of my headaches—covering up for your nymphomania, dypsomania, and lesser vices. Now it's stealing shoes."

"Shoes?" Marilyn's first startled flare of anger died. And then she stared down at the silver evening slipper still grasped defensively in her hand. She turned it over carefully and peered intently at the sole. Suddenly she smiled and relaxed all over at once, like a very demure and very sly kitten. "Oh!" It was a cute bubbling laugh. "What you must think of me!"

"Look, I'm paid to write well of you—not think well of you. So talk. And while you're about it, you might explain what you were doing out at Derwent's last night—around one."

Marilyn wriggled herself on to a studio couch, tucking one leg under her and pulling at her skirt demurely. She looked like an elfin child caught in some minor naughtiness. She smiled. "But I wasn't there."

"I saw you."

Marilyn tossed her head. "I still say I wasn't there . . . and I don't think you'll contradict it publicly. Loeb Films has a million bucks invested in me—and it's going to be protected." She waggled the shoe at him coquettishly. "And you're going to protect it."

"If I saw you—so could somebody else."

A tiny fear flickered in Marilyn's guileless eyes. "Did they?"

"I don't know—yet." Pete rubbed the barrel of the automatic absently along the arm of the chair. "So what were you doing out there—trying to get back another 'last' print of that picture?"

Marilyn gasped. "You knew he had it?"

"The police have it now."

"Oh God!" Marilyn was frightened. She huddled on the couch, nursing her knees, sucking at her full lower lip.

"How much had he asked for it this time?"

Marilyn was startled. "Was it him before? He said he got the picture from . . . Of course it was. That heel!" She glanced at Pete. "How much? Oh, a thousand. I took it out there after the première to pay him." And reading skepticism in Pete's eyes, she slapped both feet down, sat erect. "I didn't have any reason to kill him. I was going to pay him." She flung her purse at him. "The money's still in there."

Pete brushed the purse aside. "If you had shot him you could keep the money. You don't pay blackmail to a dead man."

"He was dead when I got there. Even the police had come." Marilyn gnawed at her underlip. "Will Fels do anything about the picture?"

"It wouldn't be smart for him to do anything about stuff he picked up at a blackmailer's. Besides . . ." as much as he hated to give Marilyn the pleasure he had to tell her, or she'd begin to wonder why she hadn't been questioned . . . "the face was scratched out." But he left a slight barb. "I don't think they can restore it, but they do some clever things with black light these days." That would hold her for a while. "So now let's get on to the matter of shoe-stealing."

"I'm sure she wore these shoes last night." Marilyn reached down and picked up the mate, turning it over in her hands.

"So what?"

She held out the practically new slippers. "They aren't scuffed." She seemed genuinely puzzled, but it was hard to tell about Marilyn. "And I saw someone scrambling in Germaine's window. Somebody pretty awkward." Marilyn would never be awkward. "The feet sort of clawed."

Somebody scrambling in Germaine's window! When Marilyn was there! The poisoner! Pete sat forward. "A woman?"

Marilyn shrugged. "Corliss wears slacks."

Pete laughed. "Not with evening slippers—and not at a première. It was a good try, Marilyn. What were you really after? Why the parlor maid act?" He pointed to the abandoned whisk broom.

Marilyn gnawed her lip—another of her better gestures. "I was looking for mud—dirt from around Derwent's." She frowned like a worried child. "Like I did in that mystery thing, 'Such Sweet Slaughter.' You remember. It was evidence."

"Good Lord—and what would you do with it? Analyze it?"

"Do you have to?" Marilyn looked honestly surprised. "In 'Such Sweet Slaughter' I just . . ."

"Sometimes I think you don't know where movies leave off and real life begins."

"I suppose you do!" Marilyn was swiftly venomous. "You think Corliss is so sweet—the sugar-coated lady. Well, she isn't. She knew Derwent, too." Marilyn laughed. "And well enough to have him in her dressing room." She waved away Pete's half uttered protest. "And it wasn't because she was being the gracious lady of the films, either." Marilyn's voice was honeyed with sarcasm, saccharinely sweet. "Kindly dispensing notice to a struggling young actor. Not on your life! I heard her. She told him to leave town—or she'd kill him."

"I'm afraid the lady is right. If she is a lady."

Pete whirled. Corliss Petry stood in the doorway, her young-old face calmly smiling, her gray hair softly waved, her small, spruce figure erect. One hand went out to steady herself against the door frame, as if she felt faint.

The other hand held a gun—quite steadily.

# 11

Pete was careful to keep his hand clear of the gun in his lap. He even spread his fingers and held his arms out a little from the chair so that Corliss could see them. Across him Marilyn was trying to compose her terrified face into mild, sardonic surprise, while her whole body sagged under the limp slope of her shoulders, so that she looked like a ghastly caricature of a doll that had lost its sawdust.

"Corliss . . ." Pete was wary of a woman with a gun. They were unpredictable. "Is it loaded?"

The character actress smiled at him. "Is yours?"

Marilyn answered for him. "Yes, it is, and if you don't . . ."

"Don't make threats, my dear. Not at a time like this—when I'm holding the gun. Because it would be such a pleasure to shoot you. And so nicely legal, too. You were burglarizing my dressing room." She twitched the gun sharply, and Marilyn gasped. Corliss ordered sharply, "Pete, knock the gun to the floor and kick it toward me."

Pete brushed the gun and it thudded on the floor. He shoved it with his foot, sharply, so that it spun far under the studio couch. Then he stood up—not feeling very happy about it.

"I think we've all seen too many movies. Give me that gun."

It surprised him that Corliss handed it over with a little shrug. She even smiled at him. "I'm not at all sure it is loaded. You'd better find out." Pete broke it and looked. It wasn't.

Marilyn laughed and dropped to her knees to scramble for the gun under the couch. Pete looked down. "Don't try that, Marilyn, or I'll kick you so hard you'll need a dentist to get my foot out."

The astonished star swiveled her head around and then sat protecting her threatened area. "I believe you would."

She stood up and started to sidle out, keeping clear of Pete and skirting Corliss, who had stepped into the dressing room.

"If you're thinking of running to Jake, be sure to ask to see his art gallery. It has some masterpieces. One of them cost him five thousand dollars." Pete turned away from the rage that flared in Marilyn's eyes. He dropped the gun in his pocket and motioned Corliss toward the couch. Marilyn slid out the doorway, and then he could hear her high heels clicking angrily across the dark vastness of the empty studio.

Corliss sighed and sat. "I saw a light in here." She motioned toward Pete's sagging pocket. "It's a prop gun, I think. Hammond gave it to me for this new role. He wanted me to get familiar with it."

Pete slouched down in the chair, admiring the poise and naturalness of the character actress. "If you're going to pull a gun, be sure it's ready, and be sure you're ready to use it." He stooped, fumbling under the couch for Marilyn's gun. His fingers touched it and it skidded.

"You want to know about what Marilyn told you, don't you?"

"If you want to tell me." He got the gun, straightened, and shoved it in his pocket.

"Marilyn told the truth. I did tell Derwent—or whatever his name is; he's used several—to get out of town or I'd kill him."

"He was getting out of town."

"Yes, I know. He told it around the lot that he was going to New York—for a 'personal appearance'—which of course is ridiculous. But I suppose it was as good an excuse as any. And several of the company were going. Robert Emery, for one. He left right after the première. I saw him off."

"Is that an alibi?"

"Do I need one? No, I just told you that to show where Derwent—or whoever he is—picked up his story." Corliss sat forward with Victorian correctness. "Do you really think I need an alibi?"

"Look, Corliss, I like you—a lot. And I'm a little tired of carrying around studio secrets. I'd just as soon not hear yours unless it will help to clear up this mess."

Corliss lay back against the cushions, considering. "I don't see how it can help—except that it shows what sort of man this Derwent was."

Pete grinned ruefully. "I've got an idea."

Corliss nodded. "I've known it a long time. You see, he killed my son."

"Please, Corliss . . ." Pete started to lift his hand in protest, but Corliss' voice went on.

"Davey was young and reckless—and I guess I let him have too much money." She smiled tiredly. "He was spoiled. And then this Derwent—only he called himself Andrews then; this was three years ago—this Derwent got Davey into some sort of trouble. Gambling, I think—and a girl. Down at Tia Juana. It must have been pretty sordid." She raised a hand to still the trembling of her mouth. "Davey shot himself. At least that's the story they told me." Her eyes were very far away. "Three years ago. On Lincoln's birthday. I remember, because they sent his body home on St. Valentine's Day. . . . Such a lovely Valentine for a mother." Her hand was hard against her mouth, and tears glimmered and blurred her eyes.

Pete hitched himself out of the chair and sidled out of the room, leaving Corliss Petry to memories and bitterness.

The night air was cool and the deep purple shadows of the huge studio buildings reminded him of still another duty—Patsy, and her appointment at The Blue Raven. And Bill Katon was waiting. Oh, Lord, things piled up.

And they piled up more. Tom Brady's long frame was draped on the side of the police car, his oyster-white Stetson a gigantic blob in the dark. Pete came up beside the car. Bill was gesticulating with a remnant of cold hamburger. ". . . And Pete heaved a potato into this machine gun nest—and Nips come pouring out."

Brady swung off the running board and faced Pete. "I'm right proud to own knowin' you, podner. This here hombre's been a-tellin' me . . ."

"I can imagine. Bill's very good at telling that story." He spoke to Bill. "I've got to check Dan's alibi . . ."

Brady thrust back his Stetson and scratched his head thoughtfully. "Pete, I'm wonderin' could maybe I go along . . . jess sort of ride yore trail, whilst you're doin' this here detectin'?" Brady laughed without any mirth. "I ain't never seen anybody do any real detectin', and Bill's been tellin' me . . ."

It was the laugh that did it. It wasn't sincere—and the lack of sincerity, coming from so transparent a soul as Tom Brady, was a jarring note. And jarring notes needed to be investigated. He tried to read Brady's face, but the night was too dark. He didn't want Brady with him—not at the meeting with Patsy—but Brady's persistence, his desire to hang around, was curious, and Pete wanted to dig under it. He wanted Brady handy later. He waved his hand toward the police car. "Why don't you ride with Bill—in a regular police car that's trailing a man, even if it's only me? And you can watch what I do. Not," he added for Bill's benefit, "that I'm likely to accomplish anything."

"You mean ride in a real police car?" Brady, who probably had a dozen cars, stroked the door happily. "I shore would admire to." His voice begged Bill not to turn him down.

Bill harumphed thoughtfully. "Tain't regulations." His eyes, even in the dark, were wistfully turned on Brady's gaudy outfit. "Though I can't say I remember regulations against it."

With this happy solution Pete left them and slid into his car, wondering vaguely which would outlie the other. The procession of two swung through the gates of the studio and off toward The Blue Raven.

It wasn't exactly a dump, but it didn't miss it by much. Pete could tell that from the outside. It was a corner bar, tucked in the ground floor of a shabby hotel. He got out and walked back to the police car.

"Listen, Bill. I'm meeting a girl in here." He winked. "I'd like it private." He motioned ahead. "You can pull up there and keep an eye on me through the window."

Bill leaned out the car and scowled. "Pete, this ain't the sorta dump you meet nice girls in. Now I know a place . . ."

"Mister Katon, I'm shocked!" Leaving a slightly bewildered Bill and a puzzled Brady, Pete walked into the bar. He didn't see her at first—or at least didn't recognize her. Without the dazzling brevity of her blue patent leather costume, she looked small and dumpy and plain, and he'd never have known her if she hadn't raised one plump arm and wiggled her fingers at him. Patsy grinned up at him and patted the seat beside her in the booth.

"I wasn't sure you'd make it."

Pete sidled into the booth. "I'd miss a date with a girl like you?"

Patsy nudged him sharply with her elbow and laughed. "Give that to them that likes it." But she touched the little pillbox hat into a jauntier angle. "Not but what it does a girl good to hear it." She looked up at the shoddy waiter who stood over them. "Boiler maker and his helper." She nudged Pete again. "What's yours?"

"Straight bourbon, with water and lemon juice on the side."

When the waiter had brought their drinks and gone back to lean his elbows on the bar and study a racing form, Pete lifted his drink, touched Patsy's and sipped. It wasn't bad bourbon. He looked over it at Patsy. "Were the cops rough?"

Patsy almost choked on her drink. "And did you ever see a Muldoon that couldn't hand a cop as good as ever he gave?"

"Then Fels didn't get anything out of you?"

Patsy heaved down a long slug of the beer and set her glass down. "The thin drink of water with the toothbrush breaking out on his lip?" Suddenly Patsy was demure and small and hurt. "Why, how would the likes of me know anything about a girl like that—and her only working there less than a week?" Her mouth worked sideways and she let him have the rest of it in a hoarse, low whisper. "And Dolores clammed up, too." She laughed suddenly. "Are you gonna have a time with that babe! Getting her in to meet a casting director!" Her shrewd eyes suddenly narrowed. "If you're on the level."

"I am—and don't look now, but you'll have a chance to show me how you handle the cops. Here comes one." Bill's big frame had lumbered through the door and was coming down the bar.

Pete could feel Patsy stiffen. Her eyes were hard and angry. "Bud, if this is the double-cross, they'll have to put you together with Scotch tape just to bury you."

"He's a pal." He waved at Bill, and the big detective loomed up over them, looking down uncertainly at the girl. Then he turned mildly aggrieved, hurt eyes on Pete. "Fels called me off. Said I wasted too much time on you, and he on'y wanted me to keep you outa mischief." His eyes looked hurt, puzzled. "How do I know what time you're gonna get into mischief? You got any regular schedule?" Bill remembered his hat and lifted it. "Howdy, miss." Then he bent over Pete confidentially and whispered, "What can I do with Brady? I gotta report in—and I can't with him. Not in that outfit. And he still wants to watch you being a detective."

Pete sighed. "Bring him in. I'll get rid of him later."

Bill said, "'Bye, miss," touched his hat and lumbered out.

Patsy wriggled indignantly in her seat. "Say, what is this? A private talk or a conference? And, brother, what is that?"

"That" was Tom Brady, in full cowboy regalia, two guns swinging at his hips, his oyster-white Stetson thrust back, his bandanna neckerchief loosely knotted through an ornate silver ring, his silver studded leather vest swinging open on a violent yellow and red plaid shirt. One of the men at the bar turned and started to laugh and then said loudly, "It's Tom Brady," and looked at his whiskey suspiciously. "My wife'll never believe me."

Patsy's eyes goggled, following Brady's lurching, cowboy walk, her head swiveling in anticipation of his going past their table. When he stopped, swept off his Stetson and bowed jerkily, she let out a little half-whistle, half-giggle.

"I'm shoah you'll pahdon me, ma'am, but I'd like to speak to my podner here, ma'am."

Patsy waved a plump arm airily. "Go right ahaid, podner, and don't mind me. I feel like the Oakland Ferry. Everybody's taking me for a ride tonight."

Pete waved to the opposite seat. "Sit down, Tom. This is Miss Patsy Muldoon, a friend of mine." As Brady slid eagerly into the seat, Pete signaled the for once attentive waiter. "What'll you have, Brady?"

Brady shook his head ruefully. "I nevah touch the stuff. My public won't let me." His solemn blue eyes appealed to Patsy. "My public is mostly small boys, ma'am. An' it ain't right for me to give 'em wrong ideals. Good clean livin', good sportsmanship, fair dealin' an' kindness to animals always gits a fella farther along in this world, ma'am."

Patsy stared at Brady's long, solemn face and then turned to Pete. She cleared her throat uncertainly. "He means it?" When Pete nodded she reached across the table and poked at Brady's silver-studded vest. "He's real."

Brady leaned secretively across the booth. "But you mought give me a tailor-made . . . if ain't anybody looking."

Not more than the entire bar and a good many loungers from the hotel lobby, but Pete hauled out the cigarettes, feeling that, among that particular audience, anything short of a sudden hail of bullets from Brady would seem effete. He had been annoyed with Brady for wanting to tag along—annoyed and curious. But now he was glad. Brady's flamboyant costume and colorful personality might be just the screen he needed to work behind. He settled back comfortably, quite certain that he and Patsy could talk around Brady's slow-moving mind. Patsy seemed to have grasped the possibilities, too, for she nodded.

"This couldn't be an act. You're leveling?"

"I'm as honest as Brady there."

She reached a decision. One hand dived under the table and came up, closed tightly. "I think you're a straight guy—but heaven help you if you're not." She handed him a key.

Just that—a key. A key on a scarred metal tag. A key to a hotel room. And it was this hotel—the shabby hotel where The Blue Raven sat tucked in one corner. Upstairs! Pete bounced out of the booth, to Brady's astonishment.

Pete waved vaguely. "I gotta go . . . and when you gotta go, you gotta go." Brady blushed for him.

Pete was glad Brady had made such an effective screen. His appearance in the bar had boomed business and practically emptied the lobby, so that Pete's progress to the stairs and up to the third floor was unnoticed. He stared at the key again—"327"—and matched it to a door. He stood with the key poised, listening. He couldn't hear anything, but she might be asleep. It didn't seem possible that he had found Janet West!

He slid the key into the lock and turned it, without any particular effort to be quiet. Too much quiet might startle her. He pushed open the door and stepped inside. No, no! his mind was saying. Not again! This was getting monotonous.

A woman was holding him up at the point of a gun.

# 12

She wasn't the big-eyed, terror-stricken youngster whose face he'd seen so repeatedly in that re-run newsreel. Oh, it was the same girl, all right. He recognized the wide-set eyes, deep and dark, but not too dark—a deep blue, maybe, or violet—and the mouth. How many times he had read and re-read those same soft though delicately chiseled lips.

Pete nodded, surprised at himself, at the new poise, the new strength he saw in her. She was frightened now—not terrified—not senselessly scrambling after someone—not wildly screaming.

"By the way, who is 'Hammy'?" Pete hoped it sounded casual. Apparently it didn't.

The girl's eyes opened in surprise and the gun wavered. Then she was in control again. The gun snapped up, the straight brows drew down in a small, angry scowl. So he'd said the wrong thing. Pete shrugged.

"So you've come from him." There was acid scorn in the girl's voice. "What do you want—blackmail? You ought to know by now he got it all."

Blackmail! So Derwent had had something on the kid.

"Slightly wrong, sister." Pete hitched his shoulder. "Mind if I take off my hat? I usually do." He usually didn't, but he wanted an excuse to start a movement—an excuse that wouldn't startle her into pulling that trigger. He swept one hand toward his hat and watched her eyes follow it, puzzled and wondering. She started to speak. His other hand shot out and down, the edge striking her wrist. They'd told him, in the Marines, you could bust an inch board that way. He'd never tried it with a board.

A strangled, sobbing scream as her arm jerked downward and the gun flipped away from her, and then Pete shoved, straight-arming from the shoulder. He didn't see her fly backward to the bed and up-end in a whirl of legs and tangled skirts. He regretted that, but he wanted the gun. When he straightened she was scrambling up, tucking her legs under her, one hand nursing her wrist, her eyes spitting anger, even though her lips were white with pain.

"Sorry, but I'm getting tired of being held up." He hooked a foot around a chair leg—a rather disreputable, scarred chair with an imitation leather seat and two cigarette burns. He sat straddling it, resting his arms on the top of the back, gun dangling. "Now let's get things straight."

Color was coming back to her face, the whiteness was dying out around her mouth, and the anger in her eyes was turning to bewilderment. She massaged her wrist slowly. "I haven't any more money."

"I'm not interested, Janet. That is your name, isn't it? Janet West?" As the girl started to deny it he shook his head and she nodded slowly, her lips framing a word. "No, I'm not the police. Seen the papers?" She nodded again, miserably. "Then you saw my job—the pictures of you labelled 'I Want That Girl.' I'm Jake's errand boy."

The girl's dark, deep eyes suddenly filled with tears and she turned, leaning her head against the wall, her soft mouth shaking.

While she regained control of herself he tilted up the gun and sniffed at the barrel, mentally measuring it. "Been fired and not cleaned . . . and it's a thirty-eight. Derwent was killed with a thirty-eight."

She pointed with a childish little gesture. "Oh, that gun killed him."

Pete groaned. There went a half-million dollars of Loeb Films' money. It would take that to offset the blunder of picking a murderess as a future star. "So you did the job."

The girl shook her head slightly, just enough to stir the loose brown curls. "He was dead when I got there."

"He was dead when everybody got there—so far as I can find out." Pete thrust his hat back to its usually perilous position with the barrel of the gun and then scratched his nose with it absently. "So make it good. The cops have a witness, you know, who puts you there about . . ."

"Yes. Some girl—Germaine Winters. She's a friend of Edgar's." The way she said it meant more than friend. "I never met her, and I didn't see her last night. I was too frightened." Janet shivered, remembering.

"Start from the beginning. When did you meet Derwent? How? Where?" Pete rapped the gun impatiently against the slat of the chair.

Suddenly the girl seemed to recall something. She sat up straighter. "But what's this to you? You're not police. And you're not a blackmailer. Or are you?"

"Listen, kid. I've told you. Jake had a brain child. You're it. And I'm just the doctor who stands by and sees it gets born properly. For some reason he thinks you're innocent, in spite of a lot of things. I hope you are."

"I am." Janet West said it angrily, and then her mouth softened. "Though I can see how it looks to others. You wanted me to start at the beginning? That's a long way back. In McQueeney, Texas. . . ."

"My God, is there such a place?"

The girl was indignant. "It's a wonderful little town, just out of San Antonio. It has . . ."

"Skip the statistics. And don't go too far back."

"Oh, all right. I wanted to be an actress. Not just a glamour star—an actress. And I studied. Good schools. And Hammy helped."

"I asked you once before. Who's Hammy?"

The girl frowned. "Yes, you did. That's what made me think you came from Edgar Derwent, somehow. He's the only one who knew about Hammy. Uncle Hammy. At least that's what I called him as a child—I mean when I was a child. He wanted to play Hamlet, you know."

"Most of 'em do. I mean, who wanted to play Hamlet?"

"Robert Emery. He's a star. . . ."

"Featured player," Pete corrected automatically, and then groaned. "You can't do this to me. You can't tie this any closer to Loeb Films. So Bob Emery is your uncle—and 'Hammy.' My grandmother's Aunt Harriet!"

"He isn't really my uncle—just a sort of adopted uncle. He comes from McQueeney."

"Never let that out. Not to Louella. He's strictly Groton-Harvard."

Janet's eyes were angry, her mouth set. "You Hollywood oaf! Texas has as much culture and refinement and education as . . . Oh, there isn't any point in getting angry, is there?"

"On you it looks good. But the story . . ."

"Oh yes. Uncle Bob—or Hammy—encouraged me. He wanted me to study—really study—and then he'd help me here in Hollywood. When Father died—just a few months ago—I started to come on, but there were things to be settled—mostly debts—and just about a month ago, I got everything cleared away and wrote Hammy I wanted to come now, and I sent him my photographs. I got a letter back from Edgar Derwent that he was writing for Hammy. . . ."

"Derwent? Wrote for Bob Emery? That's crazy. They never even spoke. Bob couldn't stand the guy."

The girl curled one hand upward in her lap. "But that's what he said. I've got the letter somewhere. And I came. I just had some of Father's war bonds—five of them—and some cash, but I knew Hammy would help me. Only when I got here, he was on location, and Edgar met me at the station. He was awfully nice—at first. Until I lost my bonds. And I wouldn't . . . Then he was nasty."

"I can guess what you wouldn't—and it would make Derwent sore. Then why did you go there last night?"

"Well, I'd got this job—with Patsy. Only I didn't make much, and I was behind in my room rent. Then Derwent came by Dave's and offered to take me to the première—and Hammy. He'd come back, you see, when the picture was finished. And I knew I'd never get into that crush without someone. So I went. I got off early at Dave's. Usually I was on until ten, but I got off at eight and went right out. . . ." Janet's eyes widened with the memory. "He was dead . . . lying there on the floor—dead."

"What time? Or don't you know?"

"About eight-thirty. Maybe later. Yes, I think later, because I stopped by Patsy's room here to freshen up. Maybe quarter of nine. Does it matter?"

"I don't know. I don't think they've placed the time of death that accurately. You know medical examiners—or don't you?"

Janet shivered. "No, I don't. But I know he was dead when I got there. And that gun was beside him."

"Why did you have to take it along? Why didn't you . . ."

"I was terrified. That room—all torn up. A man lying dead, and then I saw my photographs—and the bonds. Three of them. He'd stolen them. He must have. Sometime when I was out with him, because I kept them in my bag."

"He was that sort, all right. . . ." Pete looked glumly at the girl. "You know, I'm beginning to believe you. But get on with it."

"I saw my pictures, and started to pick them up. I don't know why."

"Where were these pictures?"

The girl waved her hand vaguely. "There were pictures all over. Scattered across the floor. Except for the one on his desk of a sweet-faced old lady. In a frame." She shook her head. "No, I don't guess it was there then. The desk was sort of littered with . . ." she made a little move of disgust . . . "photographs. They were ugly."

"I know the kind Derwent kept. So you picked up your photos to keep the police from identifying you. You missed one."

"I know." She shook her head firmly. "I wasn't thinking about being identified. Lots of people knew I knew Derwent. It just seemed something to do to keep from looking at him. And then I heard something—somebody. At the front door. And I got panicky. I kept thinking maybe it was the murderer coming back. I grabbed up the gun and slipped out the back way. As soon as I'd done it, I knew it was a mistake—but I was confused. All I could think about was getting away from there and getting to Hammy at the première. Only they wouldn't let me through. I tried. . . ."

"We've got that on film. And that's why I believe your story." Pete stood up, dropping the gun in his pocket. He seemed to be making a collection. "I'll keep this till I can think of a way to get rid of it."

The girl studied her hands in her lap, rubbed her wrist thoughtfully. "Why does that picture make you think my story is true? Does it prove anything?"

Pete shook his head. "Not a thing. Except that I can't figure any other story screwy enough to account for a frightened girl yelling 'Hammy, Hammy, Hammy' at a première."

# 13

When Pete got back to the bar, Dan Kelley looked up from leaning into the booth.

If Patsy was impressed by playing hostess to a famous star and well-known character actor, she didn't show it. She flipped a hand at Kelley. "He drinks standing up."

"He drinks—period." And Kelley finished a whiskey sour at a gulp. "Especially if it's on a Loeb Films expense account."

"It is." Pete picked up the check and, reading the question in Patsy's eyes, winked solemnly. "And we're leaving."

"If you're checking my alibi, I wasn't in this bar last night." He looked around, his ugly face drawn in a scowl. "But it's probably the only one I wasn't in."

"This was just pleasure." Pete nodded to Patsy, and she winked back. "But from now on, it's business." He paid the slouching waiter and they started out.

"I'm going along," Kelley announced belligerently, as if he expected to be contradicted. "After all, it's my alibi."

Pete had to fend off Tom Brady's awkward efforts to help Patsy out of the booth and, with his hand under her arm, he slipped her the hotel key. As she got out she straightened—or anyway adjusted—the pillbox hat. She smiled at the three men. "A girl has to, too." And she disappeared into the hotel's microscopic lobby.

Brady, leaning against the side of Pete's car, was still obviously in the mood to discuss something with Pete—but Kelley was there.

Patsy swished out of the hotel—Pete noted the inappropriate name, "Le Grand"—and stopped to whistle softly. "Some bus." She grinned at Pete. "Maybe I *should* get in the movies." She climbed in the front seat with a purposefulness that compelled Brady and Kelley to slide past her into the cramped rear. Pete started off, accepting Kelley's directions.

"We left the première and went right out Sunset." A moment later he tapped Pete's shoulder. "We stopped there—Spigotti's place." It was just a bar. It made no effort toward freakishness, no attempt to be an igloo or a champagne bucket or derby hat. Pete recognized Carlo himself with one leg thrown over a bar stool, careful of the fit of his double-breasted suit. Carlo was a little too well known on the fringes of the movie world—as a gambler and bookie. Pete himself had placed bets through him, and he suspected that in the two floors above the bar there was plenty of gambling equipment. It wouldn't be operating this early. In fact, the bar itself was nearly empty.

The four of them started into a booth, and Pete looked at Kelley. "You sure this is the place? Is your waiter here?"

"We stood at the bar."

Pete swerved and the others trailed him, lining up against the bar. A bartender, who moved as if his feet hurt, came down to stand in front of them, his eyes on Brady's silver-studded vest curiously. "What'll it be?"

"That him?"

Kelley nodded. "Yeah, that's the guy."

The bartender's pickled-onion eyes swiveled from Brady and centered on Kelley. "What's the beef?" One hand was reaching under the bar for something—Pete suspected a blackjack. "If this guy claims . . ."

"This isn't a squawk, buddy. This guy is just trying to remember where he was last night."

The bartender didn't relax. He just shook his head. "He didn't lose nothing here."

"But he was here?"

A hand tapped Pete's shoulder and he turned to see Carlo Spigotti's dark face thrust close—calm, without any menace. "You heard Gus. He didn't lose anything. Ain't that enough?"

"He doesn't claim to have lost anything. Except maybe his memory. For a couple of hours. Sort of mislaid it. Was he here?"

The barkeep stared past Pete, watching Carlo. The gambler nodded and the bar man relaxed. "Yeah. He was here. With a party. Plastered."

"What time?"

Again the barman looked at Carlo before he answered. "Should I keep tabs on all the drunks?" He shrugged. "After eleven. Before midnight. I'm off at midnight."

Carlo tapped Pete's shoulder again. "What's this about?" His face wasn't so calm, but there was still no menace. "Getting times—that sounds like an alibi." His dark eyes narrowed and he swung them to Kelley, raking the actor from head to foot. "You're in pitchers. You're Dan Kelley." His eyes flickered over the others, settling on Pete. "And for you, bud, this is a tip. Don't mess around in Derwent's affairs. See?"

"Thanks." Pete edged around the gambler, smiling. "You've made a mistake, Carlo. We've got all we wanted to know—originally. You see, then I didn't know you were interested in Derwent. But thanks for the tip."

The gambler's eyes were suddenly hot and angry and his lips curled back over startling white teeth. Then he shrugged. "It still goes. Don't mess around."

Pete nodded pleasantly and followed the others out. "Dan, where's the next stop?"

"Out near Derwent's. It's called—I think—Bogart's. It's just ahead."

It was—a neighborhood tavern undistinguished by even its distinguishing neon sign. Pete chuckled. "How come you remembered?"

Dan leaned his arms on the back of the seat, resting his chin on them. "The name. Bogart. And me. Bogarts a tough guy. I'm a tough guy. We're both in the movies. I think somebody commented on it. Anyway, I remember Derwent's name was struck up there—because I commented on that."

They walked in. Bogart's wasn't quite as deserted as Carlo's had been. It was a neighborhood place and the neighbors were gathering. They sat, some of them five and six to a booth, and the groups called back and forth to each other. A genial place. And the bartender suited it. He leaned fat arms on the bar and nodded his several chins at a solitary beer drinker. "I'm from Brooklyn, m'self, and I sorta miss the Dodgers." He looked up at Pete's signal. "What'll it be, gents?"

They ranged themselves just beyond the beer drinker and ordered. Pete swung around on his stool and looked the place over. The staggered name plates, clumsily lettered, ranged above the wall brackets for hats and coats. And Derwent's was there. So Dan did remember. When Pete turned back, the bartender was smiling.

"Little idea of mine. Folks like to see their names up there. Keeps 'em comin' back—and don't cost much."

"It's a good idea—good psychology."

"I don't know about psychology. I just know folks." He polished the bar industriously. "Seems to get me just about as far."

"Know that guy?" Pete aimed his thumb at Kelley and the bartender turned, squinting.

"Yeah. He's in the movies, ain't he? We get some movie folks, onct in a while. Not stars. Just movie folks."

"Ever see him before? I don't mean in movies. In here?"

The bartender leaned on a fat elbow and peered at Dan, nodding so that the pink accordion of his chins opened and folded back. "Yeah." And then with more conviction, "Yeah. Last night. And boy, was he plastered." He shook his head sadly. "I don't like to see 'em plastered. It's bad for business. Folks should drink moderate." He thought that over. "Moderate—but steady. Regular I mean. Every evening. A little. Keeps 'em mellow and friendly." The barkeep was having difficulty keeping his eyes off Brady's gaudy outfit, but he was politely ignoring it. "Helps their digestion too. I like to see folks . . . Say, ain't that Tom Brady?" He moved down the bar to Brady's place, holding out a broad pink hand. "Tom Brady, ain't you?"

Brady grasped the hand and then looked nervously around to make sure that none of his "public"—the small fry—had caught him in a bar. "Yeah." He pointed hastily to the drink. "But this is lemonade."

"I know." The bartender didn't sound quite so happy. "I fixed it." He relinquished Brady and came back to Pete—but reluctantly. "What is it, bub?"

"Would you know what time that guy was in here last night?"

The bartender concentrated on Dan for a moment, and then brightened. "Yeah . . . I think so. Now let me see . . ." He caught two of his chins and mauled them thoughtfully. "There was another guy in here earlier. Movie folks, too. Maybe you know him—plays with that Marilyn Courtney." The bartenders eyes danced at that. "Is she a dish!"

"Charles Abbott?" Pete wondered vaguely why Abbott should be way out here in this obscure bar. He preferred the glitter of nightclubs—especially those with m.c.'s who pointed out celebrities. "What was he doing here?"

The bartender resented the implication. "This is a nice little joint." As Pete made soothing noises, indicating his firm belief in the niceness of the joint, the bartender calmed down. "He come here to get swowzled. Friend of his just died. That feller there." The bartender pointed a blunt, broken-nailed finger. "Maybe you read about it. This actor—was he busted up."

Pete stared at the name the bartender pointed out—Derwent. And Charles Abbott had known last night that Derwent was dead! Before Dan Kelley found the body. "Just a minute." He tapped the barkeep's fat shoulder. "Are you sure Abbott was in here before that guy?" He nodded to Kelley.

The bartender drew back scornfully. "Am I sure? Look, this guy comes in, laughing—but not exactly laughing—if you get what I mean—about one of my regulars being dead. I guess I remember that. And then this guy shows up. Maybe ten minutes later—after this first guy has lapped up four straight ryes—and is *he* swowzled! He and this dame. And is she a dish! And a couple of others. And then he starts to talk about going to see Derwent. I don't think they're in no condition to go calling where there's been a death in the family, but that ain't my job, see. So I don't say anything. Ony this morning, I read in the papers this Derwent don't just die. He's been kill't—and this guy Kelley found him." The bartender leaned his fat face between two ham-like fists and peered thoughtfully over Pete's shoulder. "On'y if this guy, Kelley, finds the body, how come the first guy knew he was dead? I don't get it. . . ."

"I wouldn't try," Pete hastily assured him. "They do things like that in the movies all the time. It's really simple."

The bartender blinked thoughtfully and then looked relieved. He straightened. “Yeah—the movies. I guess you’re right. That’ll be two ten for the drinks and twenty for the lemonade.”

# 14

Pete climbed into the convertible before he realized a not too subtle change had been rung on him. Dan sat in front and Patsy and Tom in the rear—from which was coming a not very enthusiastic account of Tom's horse and his complete lack of desire to kiss it again.

Pete leaned confidentially toward Dan. "Can't you get the oaf out of here? After all, I have a date with that kid."

Dan glanced over his shoulder. "You *had* a date with that kid." He grinned wryly and shrugged. "I'll do what I can—but how do I go about luring him? With a lump of sugar? He won't drink. . . ."

"Tell him you know a speakeasy where they serve tailor-mades."

"Do I? What the devil are they?"

"His secret vice. Chesterfields. He can't roll his own."

Dan nodded and leaned into the back of the car. "Hey, Tom, let's break this up. We're riding herd on Pete's date."

With a rumble of apologies Brady heaved himself forward, and Pete swung the car to the curb, near the studio gates.

"Jes' put me down here, podner. . . ." His long, booted legs slid over the seat, and he followed Dan to the sidewalk and then turned back to shake Pete's hand. "I'm sorry, podner." His big, solemn face was screwed into actual worry.

"I wasn't tryin' to horn in on yore date, podner." His voice went confidential—a husky bellow not audible to a deaf man more than a block away. "But that's a mighty pert gal you got there. Don't let nothin' happen to her."

Pete vowed she'd be intact and spurted away as Patsy scrambled over the back of the seat, giggling. "He's cute, ain't he?" She settled herself with a shake and a tug at her skirt, while Pete headed for The Blue Raven once more.

When they were almost there Patsy touched his arm. "She didn't do it, Pete."

Patsy nodded. "Most men look like hell from the rear. . . ."

"Thanks, Patsy. And here we are. How do we work this? Do you go up first, and I follow?"

Patsy sneered at the hotel. "In that dump? It doesn't pay to bother. Just come in with me." She slid out of the car and he followed. Beyond a casual but somehow calculating stare and a smirk, the desk clerk said nothing. And Pete's second journey down the narrow, stuffy corridor was uninterrupted, though the place gave him a guilty feeling, just from the smell of it.

Patsy started to use the key and then looked over her shoulder, pushing open the door. "Unlocked."

Pete thrust past her into the room. The naked bulb lighted the small room garishly, showing up the cheap maple furniture in all its raw ugliness. It wasn't kind to the sleazy cretonne curtains or the faded jaspé covers on the daybed. Nothing was disarranged except a single cushion that stood stiffly upright. Even the bedside radio played tirelessly on.

And Janet West was gone.

Unless . . . Sick at his stomach, Pete whirled to the closet and yanked open the door. A few dresses and scraps of Patsy's uniforms hung slackly in the narrow space. He turned back to the girl, ignoring her stricken face. "Bathroom?"

"Down the hall. We don't run to private baths." She let that trail as she scudded out.

Pete kicked the chair around and sat down, arms on its back, scanning the room. If a girl just went to the bathroom, would she leave everything so orderly? There should be something just casually laid down—a book, a newspaper.

Patsy was back, her eyes darting around the room . . . "She's not there." She walked over and started to straighten the upright pillow. "I don't like . . ." It died in a soft squeak. "Pete!"

He knocked over the chair getting to her and looked down at the vacant space. Not quite vacant. The edge of a black leather pocketbook showed. He reached for it. "Hers?"

Patsy swallowed once and nodded. "She'd never leave it without a reason. A girl doesn't . . ."

Pete was already looking through it. The war bonds were there—three of them. And a letter addressed to Janet in McQueeney, Texas—from Edgar Derwent. He didn't stop to read it. Lipstick, powder, handkerchief, a bottle of perfume. A girl wouldn't leave those things. Even Pete knew that. Not willingly.

"Fels! He's got her! Somehow that son of a . . ."

Music on the radio died and an artfully excited voice came on. "Flash! Germaine Winters, star witness in the double murder of Edgar Derwent and Virginia Struthers last night, was found shot to death at eight-twenty this evening, in a vacant lot on Van Nuys Avenue. Miss Winters was released earlier tonight from the Hollywood district jail on bail furnished by her employer, Peter Hack. Assistant District Attorney Bynum Fels has issued a pick-up order for Peter Hack, described as a press agent for Loeb Films. The police description follows: Six feet one inch, sandy hair, blue eyes . . ." Pete reached over and snapped off the radio, and then looked at his hand. It was shaking.

"Baby . . ." Pete whirled on Patsy, thrust the black leather bag under her arm and caught her free hand. "We need alibis—but bad! Come on. Downstairs. . . ."

They scurried down to the bar and sidled in to a booth. Pete ordered drinks and they sat for a few moments toying with them. Pete didn't want his. He wanted a clear head. And Patsy didn't seem to be able to swallow her boiler maker and his helper. Gradually Pete became conscious of the radio playing. It was the same interrupted program they had heard upstairs. He looked up. "Patsy, we heard it in this bar." As she looked blank he pointed to the loud-speaker on the wall. "The radio—the announcement. And we're going down to see Fels. Or I am."

Patsy was already sliding out of the seat. "Me too."

He paid the bill and they walked out to the car. Pete helped Patsy in and then went around to the driver's seat. He was just stooping over to unlock the car when he heard a voice at his shoulder.

"Don't touch it!"

Pete' straightened slowly and turned. Russell's heavy pudding face was visible in the neon glow from the bar, and it was grinning. "Planning a getaway, huh? Fugitive from justice."

"Cut it, Russell. . . ." Fels' elegant slimness loomed beside him and the big detective moved aside. Fels was smiling nastily. "I'm sure Mister Hack is anxious to co-operate."

Pete nodded. "Matter of fact, I was on my way to see you."

"Remarkable coincidence. I was on my way to see you. Katon told me he left you here. At seven, or thereabouts." He peered through the car at The Blue Raven. "Been there ever since?"

"Nup. This was a round trip. We just got back and heard you wanted me. Radio."

Fels touched his hat to Patsy and then scowled. "Haven't I seen you somewhere before? Recently."

Pete didn't want the assistant D.A. to tie Patsy to Dave's Drive-In—and Janet West, so he nodded hastily. "Probably at the studio. When you were questioning us there. My secretary."

"Oh!" Fels looked thoughtfully blank. "Oh, yes."

"And what's this about me putting up bail for Germaine?" Attack, with Fels, was a good method of confusion. "You know I never put up bail for Germaine. I wanted her in jail. She was safe there."

Fels backed away from the attack, held up a hand. "That's what the desk sergeant said, Hack. I know Katon said you never went anywhere near Headquarters, but. . ." He looked distressed. "I gotta trust my own men, haven't I? Only which one?"

"Look. . . ." Pete wanted this over in a hurry. He wanted to be free of Fels—free to begin anew the hunt for the elusive Janet West. "I've got witnesses to account for every minute of my time. Independent witnesses. Brady and Kelley."

Fels snorted. "They'd stooge for Tobias and you any day."

"And three bartenders, waiters, and assorted customers. We made a tour of the bars between here and Derwent's."

Fels' eyes narrowed and his face thrust closer. "Here and Derwent's? Why?"

Pete fumbled for a cigarette. "I was checking Kelley's alibi." He grinned at the assistant D.A. "Because I knew you'd want it sometime soon." He gave it to Fels slowly, omitting Charles Abbott's curious and too early knowledge of the murder. "I'm leveling with you, Fels. Kelley couldn't have killed Derwent."

"I didn't think so much of that idea, anyway." Fels caught his lower lip in his fingers and twisted. "We know he was killed early in the evening, between eight and nine, which eliminates nearly everybody who was at the première except the girl—Janet West. But right now I'm worried about who got Germaine . . . and if you've an alibi . . ." He opened the door of the convertible and slid into the back seat. "We can check it quick." He leaned out. "Russell, follow in my car."

Pete retraced their route and drew up before Carlo Spigotti's discreet bar, and the three of them went in. It was still a little early for Spigotti's clientele and the dim interior was almost bare, except for Gus behind the bar and Carlo lounging near the door. It didn't seem to have changed in the past hour and a half. Pete went up to the bar and signaled Gus, who moved as if his feet still hurt. Gus came opposite them. "What'll it be?"

Pete leaned on the bar. "Remember me? I was in here earlier, around seven-thirty." There was nothing in the pickled-onion eyes—just blankness. "With a guy in a cowboy outfit, another guy, and this young lady." He waved a hand at Patsy.

The bartender reached down for glasses, set three along the bar. "I see a lot of people. What'll it be?"

Carlo moved down the bar, came up behind them.

"Something wrong, Gus?" His eyes flickered over Pete, slid over Patsy, and studied the assistant district attorney. "Can I help you?"

Patsy spoke up. "We were in here before. Remember? Asking about. . ." Pete touched her arm and she shut up.

He turned to Carlo, noticing the tightness around his mouth and the dark, mocking glitter in his eyes. And across Carlos well-padded shoulder he could see Fels looking skeptical.

Fels tapped the gambler's shoulder, and Carlo turned jerkily. "Were these people in here earlier? Around seven-thirty?"

Carlo smiled. "You see how empty the place is." He shrugged. "It's always like this until late. Hasn't been anybody in here this evening." He smiled tightly. "A man in a cowboy suit? Perhaps it is one of these new games they play. I'd certainly remember that. I've been here all evening." He shrugged. "It must have been some other bar." He started away. "There are so many. Serve the party, Gus."

Fels glared at Pete, his eyes narrowing. He didn't need to say anything. Pete could read his disbelief all too clearly.

"Might as well have a drink while were here. What'll yours be, Fels?"

The assistant D.A. hesitated and then swung a neatly trousered leg over a bar stool. "Scotch and water."

Gus came abruptly to life, diving below the bar to produce a bottle. He glanced inquiringly at Patsy.

"Boiler maker and his helper." It was a low dispirited order.

"And you can make mine the same as I had before." Pete slouched on the bar.

"Bourbon and water with lemon juice." Gus grinned and turned away.

"Thanks for remembering." Pete said it quietly.

The broad back of the bartender stiffened and he turned to glare at Pete. Fels was reaching for a swizzle stick; his hand paused and then went on. He even managed a low chuckle. "Neat. Very neat." And swished his Scotch with concentrated thoroughness.

Gus finished serving them, but he had lost a bartender's sure, deft touch and liquor splashed on the bar, while his eyes kept turning toward the door through which Carlo had disappeared.

Pete sipped at his drink, set it down and nodded toward the door. "You can tell the boss it isn't necessary to tip off the police I'm here." He nodded sidewise at Fels.

"He's police. The assistant district attorney. I think Carlo would like to know."

Gus gave him a long and not very loving look before he scuttled down the bar and through the door.

Pete finished his drink and signaled the others. "I'll leave the money for these. There's no need to embarrass Carlo, and I've a notion a visit from the assistant district attorney will be very embarrassing." He moved to the door. "But it's interesting to know somebody is trying to sabotage my alibi."

# 15

Bogart's Bar and Tavern had stepped up to a lively tempo. Two couples were dancing to a raucous juke box in spite of a "No Dancing" sign, and several groups at the tables were attempting to sing either that song or another, it didn't seem to matter particularly. The jovial barkeeper sidled away from what was probably an interminable story, nodding vaguely back at the drunken teller and trying to beam at his new guests at the same time.

"And what'll it be, folks?" His eyes finally relinquished the story teller and focused on Pete. "Well, hello, feller. And you, miss. Where's your friends? Lose 'em?" A phone rang back in a booth and the jovial bartender yelled to somebody named Ducky to get it. He swabbed the bar enthusiastically and beamed. "Same as before?" His merry, fat-folded eyes swept Fels. "And yours?"

"For you, Charlie!" A head protruded from the phone booth and bellowed.

The bartender beamed. "'Scuse me." He waddled off, ducking under an opening in the bar that didn't seem big enough but apparently was. He squeezed into the phone booth and closed the door, so that they could see the upper segment of him nodding at the wall phone.

Fels backed himself on to a bar stool and looked at Pete. "Well, this one remembers you. So maybe you do have an alibi." Fels laughed. "I wasn't really serious about you, Hack. But I've got to check up. And you stuck out in this like a sore thumb." Fels waved away Pete's protest. "Oh, maybe not you personally. But you'd do anything for your boss . . ."

"Sure. I don't feel like my day's complete until I've committed my quota of murders. All Jake has to do is point . . ."

Fels snorted. "Bosh! And I don't mean that. But you do do your darnedest to suppress evidence and. . . ."

"And stubborn witnesses and commit a little burglary and a trifle of arson . . . But here comes my alibi . . . Hi, Charlie . . ."

The stout bartender heaved himself down the bar and looked at Pete with carefully blank eyes. "Something for you? What'll it be, folks?" A faint twitch of a smile started and died.

Pete tapped his own chest. "Remember me? And the friends I didn't bring back? The ones . . ." Pete's voice trickled off and died. Obviously Charlie wasn't remembering anything. His eyes were too studiously staring through Pete's tie.

"What'll it be, gents?" His voice was a gulpy creak.

"Hey!" Fels had caught the strained atmosphere. He leaned across the bar. "Just a minute ago you mentioned this man and his friends. . . ."

Charlie's eyes studied a swirling electric fan. "Must have been thinking of somebody else. I never saw this guy before in my life."

"Now look here . . ."

Fels leaned threateningly across the counter, but Pete hauled him back. "Come on, Fels. Rounds one and two go against Pete." And then Pete leaned over and caught Charlie's shirt front, jerking the fat man close against the counter so that he couldn't reach under it for the inevitable blackjack. "But, Charlie, just remember—it's the last round that counts." He gave the fat man a quick, angry thrust that sent him staggering back among his bottles, his arms flailing in a frantic effort to keep his balance. A bottle crashed down.

Several of the customers had turned and were craning out of the booths. Two men stood up and started toward them. Fels whipped out a badge from his pocket, held it up.

"Police."

The men stopped and looked uneasily at each other and then at Charlie, who had gone gray, his little cherub mouth quivering.

"You still don't remember?" Pete didn't even wait for Charlie's headshake to start. He knew what the answer would be.

The three of them walked out.

Russell sidled up. "Say, Chief. What's the idea of the tail? Don't you trust me?"

"Don't be a . . . Tail?" Fels whirled to glance down the street. "Was there a tail on you?"

"Been a coupé following me ever since we left that last place. I thought maybe you put a . . ."

"Where? Where's the . . ."

"When you went in there, this coupé went scooting by and around the corner."

"And you didn't follow it? Why, you . . ."

"But, Chief . . ."

Pete edged in. He jerked a thumb toward the bar. "Coming like that, it could tie up with the phone call Charlie got. The one that froze my alibi." He glanced at Russell. "The coupé started tailing you at Carlo's?"

"Was that Carlo's? That last place? Yeah." Russell seemed to feel he'd said too much and started backing away, because Fels was glaring.

Fels slapped the brim of his hat twice and then motioned to Russell. "Follow us. I'm giving this guy one more chance."

They drove on out toward Brady's valley ranch, "Phantom Corral," where Fels made them wait in the car while he went in alone. In a few minutes he came out, Brady's long, lanky figure striding beside him.

Brady came to lean on the side of Pete's car. "Howdy, podner. 'Pears you been in trouble. But I fixed that with the sheriff."

Fels winced at "the sheriff" but shook hands with Brady, waved a good-bye to Pete and Patsy, and went off grumpily with Russell.

Brady bowed himself half into the convertible. "I'm extendin' the simple hospitality of 'Phantom Corral,' ma'am, an' I'd be mighty proud if you'd accept." He waved an extravagant gesture, spoiled somewhat by cracking his knuckles on the windshield.

Pete swung out of the car. "Come on, Patsy. Maybe you can help me dope out what happened to Janet. . . ."

In the huge, low-ceiled room Patsy whistled softly and clutched at Brady's arm. "Which end do the Indians live in?"

"Why, ma'am, there ain't been any Indians 'round these parts since . . ." Brady grinned slowly—a homely, friendly grin. "Why, ma'am, I do believe you're joshing me." His solemn blue eyes surveyed the long, cool room. "It does git pow'ful lonesome, with nobody but me and m'hosses."

Pete sank down on one of the lounges, looking up at the plump, dynamic Patsy and the long, slow Westerner, and grinned. And then, not so much to get Brady's intelligence on the problem—an effort he felt certain would not be worth the result—but to clarify it for himself, Pete outlined the story of Janet to date . . . to her disappearance from the hotel room. Somebody had gotten her—and it wasn't Fels. Fels would have gloated.

Patsy and Brady offered suggestions, not very helpful suggestions, ranging from Patsy's not very optimistic offering of white slavers to Brady's apparently unrelated notion of a secret door. "Why I remember, in one of my pictures . . ."

Pete wasn't listening. He was talking—thinking out loud. "It could be. Carlo was certainly gumming up my alibi . . . and it wasn't because he didn't want the police nosing around. He'd have got rid of them quicker if he'd told the truth. He must have heard the news about Fels wanting me and . . . that's it. He wanted the police to hold me. He wanted me out of the way. Why?"

"That no-count half-breed . . . he's yore man. Why, I remember in one picture, a cattle rustler kidnapped the girl, and I chased right into his . . ."

"In your picture, the cattle rustler always kidnaps the girl."

Brady looked hurt. "Why, in one, it was the crooked sheriff done the kidnapping."

Kidnapping! It made a crazy sort of sense. But why Carlo? Unless Carlo was the murderer. Pete bounded up. That could be it. Carlo had warned him to stay out of Derwent's affairs. Carlo had done his best to wreck Pete's alibi. Carlo had . . .

Pete was in his car before he had really completed the thought. Brady, while he was talking, had vanished somewhere, and Patsy came running across the ranch patio. At that moment Brady's huge touring car, an immense yellow job with a heavily throbbing motor, spurted around the corner. Pete held open the door of his car for Patsy. "Climb in."

Patsy shook her head and started for Brady's car. "I've always wanted to ride in a battleship on wheels, and I might as well now, if I've got to die."

That sobered Pete a little. He hadn't stopped to think what tackling Carlo would mean—especially if the man was a murderer—and then the thought of Janet West, frightened and in his hands, drove the momentary caution from his mind. He roared down the road toward the city, vivid yellow headlights swinging out to follow.

Only they didn't follow. With a full-throated bellow of the touring car's imported motor, Brady flashed past, despite Pete's frantic jockeying. And from then on it was a race—a hopeless, wild, hysterical race into the Los Angeles suburbs, with Pete's convertible no match for Brady's yellow peril—and Brady's movie-chase mind behind the wheel.

Even so, Pete wasn't more than a minute behind the big yellow car when he drew up a block from Spigotti's place. Pete slammed on the brakes, flung open the door and lit running, his several pistols banging around his hips. Pistols! He'd forgotten his collection. He reached down, clawing at one swaying pocket as he ran. He passed the motionless yellow car, and Patsy leaned out. "Pete! He's crazy! He's in there."

Pete whipped through the discreet dark door—and stopped. Brady stood spraddle-legged in the center of the barroom, two pistols moving with snakelike ferocity to cover Gus, the bartender with sore feet, a waiter who looked ready to collapse of weariness or fear, and Carlo Spigotti. They stood back against the rear wall, hands at ear level.

"I've come to git the girl."

Carlo smiled slowly. "We didn't figure on you, boy scout. But we were looking for your friend. He's here now. . . ."

Pete heard a movement behind him, and started to turn. Somebody hit him. He felt, even as he went down, that it was a dirty trick. Hit him with a sap . . . and the lights went out.

# 16

Pete felt that it wasn't fair for Tom Brady to grow so much. He was nineteen feet high and he swayed like a pendulum.

He knew where they were. Upstairs, over Carlo's discreet bar—in the gambling room, closed for tonight. And Tom Brady was leaning against the wall, slowly shaking his head. That was what added to the illusion of swaying. He wished Tom would stop shaking his head; it started his stomach heaving again.

"Stop shaking your head." Tom gave it a final shake and blinked.

"We been took, podner."

Somewhere behind Pete somebody laughed. Very slowly Pete rolled over and looked up at Carlo Spigotti. Even looking at him upside down didn't improve his appearance. Gus, the bartender with sore feet, was resting his broad rump on a shrouded roulette table, wriggling his toes and looking over, one by one, a collection of guns.

A door behind Pete opened and one of Carlo's men stuck his head in. "Nobody else outside. Got 'em all."

Pete felt a lurching in his insides. He'd figured on Patsy.

"Okay. Now bring in the girl and we'll get busy." Carlo grinned down at Pete. "And we'll also see who's a smart crook."

"You're going to a lot of trouble, Carlo, just to cover up killing a slug like Derwent. You might have got away with that, but now it's Virginia, and Germaine, and a kidnapping rap and . . ."

"You're so kind to tell me, only I don't need advice. I'm running this show from now on." He grinned as if he were enjoying something tasty. "Yeah—from now on." He went over to the table and looked over Gus' collection of guns, picking up Brady's two huge Colts and weighing them. He stared across at the cowboy. "You like heavy artillery." He dropped them on the table and picked up Corliss' gun. "Fancy—but light." He dropped it and weighed Marilyn's. "Not my speed. Now this . . ." He picked up the gun Pete had taken from Janet. "This is a handy gun. . . ." He scowled toward the door and then motioned with the gun to Pete. "Don't you stand up when a lady comes in?"

Pete moved smoothly and easily, getting up. He waved a little salute to Janet, who stood in the doorway, hands hidden behind her, her eyes blinking in the glare of the overheads. She saw him and smiled shyly. "You found me."

"And so did I, baby. Don't forget that." Carlo laughed.

"I've been wondering about that."

"Simple." Carlo lighted a cigarette from the stub and ground out the butt on the thick carpet. "I spotted Patsy. And I remembered her from Dave's. She's a nice kid, all right, but Pete . . ." Carlo shrugged. "Not the girl for a guy that's got all of Loeb studio dames to pick from. So there musta been a reason for you hanging onto her."

Tom lurched away from the wall, and Carlo swung the gun. "Stay there, boy scout."

Tom sank back against the wall, muttering. "Patsy is a fine woman. And if you was to harm a hair of her head . . ."

"All I wanted was her address." Carlo laughed. "I got it from Dave, and the rest was easy." He waved the gun to demonstrate how easy.

Pete heard a roar and a crash, and felt the room jump and lurch. And then the tinkling of glass and a man's wild shriek.

"Earthquake!" Carlo screamed out the word and lunged toward the door, waving the gun. "Get back! Get back!"

A man's white face showed at the head of the stairs. "Boss! A car came right through the window!"

Carlo checked his wild plunge and turned back. "Cover 'em, Gus. Keep 'em here while I . . ." He and the man bolted down the stairs.

Gus slid off the table and grabbed for one of the guns. But not quickly enough. One of Pete's heels crushed down on the fat man's sore foot, and Gus screamed, doubling up. Pete felt his fist swinging automatically, felt the soft thud as it caught the man in the stomach and stuck momentarily in the flabby flesh. Gus twitched once and started to fall. Pete's other hand chopped down on the fat roll of his neck, and Gus sighed heavily, flung out his arms and hit the floor with a sodden thud, out cold.

By the time Pete straightened, Brady had scooped up his two guns and was at the head of the stairs. Pete caught up the remaining two guns and started after him, prodding a bewildered Janet along with his elbow. He didn't have time to untie her hands. He dropped one gun in his pocket and caught her arm to steady her.

"Not that way, Tom. There's a back way out. Bound to be. . . ." He raced for the back of the long gambling room, sure that such a place would have a second exit. It did. He flung open the door and stared down a steep flight of stairs. A light at the bottom showed the kitchen—empty as far as he could tell. He looked back. Tom was covering their retreat, backing toward them, guns trained on the door at the head of the front stair.

Pete helped Janet stumblingly down the steep stairs and peered into the kitchen. The excitement up front had drawn the help—if any—and the big, shadowed room was bare. He felt Brady behind him and whispered back over his shoulder, "The back door. Should be an alley. The cars are a block north."

The three scuttled across the floor, hearing behind them excited, shrill voices and trampling feet, muttered curses—and in the distance, the rising wail of a police siren. The door had a bolt, but gave easily—and they were out in the night, running down a dark, littered alley, toward the lighter darkness of a side street. Across the street and into shadows cast by the trees—and then Pete slowed, his breath coming gulpily. He was conscious suddenly of the soft warmth of Janet's body where his arm was tucked under hers. He pulled it out, almost angry with himself for noticing. He fished up a penknife and turned her around, sawing at the gauze bandage that bound her wrists. It parted, unravelling, and she moved her arms gratefully, with little rocking movements of her shoulders. He didn't give her time to limber up, but pushed her on ahead, around the corner, and started toward the cars.

Only there weren't cars there—not cars. Just one. Just Pete's convertible. Brady's yellow monster was gone. Pete almost laughed. He didn't need to look back down the boulevard to know that the long yellow snout was plunged deep into the plate glass window of Carlo's once discreet bar.

Tom, however, was looking, his jaw hanging. "That pore gal cain't drive a car." He started off at a lope. "If that gal's hurt. . ." His guns were still out, ready for instant action.

Pete caught his arm. "Put 'em up." Tom lowered his guns reluctantly. "She did it deliberately, Brady—to save us. And if that voice I hear screaming at the police and everybody else is whose I think it is, she isn't hurt."

Down the street, in front of Carlos place, there was a jackstraw huddle of police cars, nosed in around the yellow monster projecting out across the sidewalk. Other cars were arriving now—the ordinary hodge-podge of curiosity seekers. And among them, Pete felt he could find anonymity. He bustled Tom toward the convertible and motioned Janet into the rear seat. "And keep down."

He started the car and drove into the edge of the jam around the police cars, standing up to peer at the shattered front of the bar . . . and Patsy standing high on the back seat of the yellow touring car, hands on her hips, her head wagging furiously. A policeman below her was frantically trying to reach her, and she evaded him neatly, slapping aside his hands. ". . . And furthermore, I'm not drunk! My man's in there, and I'm getting him out."

Pete could see Carlo hopping around as if the sidewalk had suddenly got hot. "Officer, I tell you I'm not pressing any charges. It was an accident. . . ."

"Accident, nothing. I meant to do it, you wall-eyed wallaby. And I want my man. . . ."

"An accident . . ." Carlo stepped on the running board and reached for Patsy. One flailing hand caught him in the eye and he fell back, swearing.

"Get in there, Tom, and square things. And quick. Carlo won't dare make a fuss. If you have to, go to the precinct station with the cops and send a wrecker for the car. But get Patsy away from there. Pay her fine—post bond—call the studio lawyer—but get her out. I've got to get Janet away from here. We'll be at the studio—my office. I'll phone the lawyer—but get Patsy out of there. Now!"

Tom Brady thrust his big Stetson far back on his head and swung out of the car, striding toward the center of disturbance. "I'm here, honey. I'm a-comin'."

Patsy looked out over the crowd, the tangled police cars, and spotted Tom wading through the mob toward her. As he reached the side of the big yellow car she flung up her hands and dived at him. "My hero!"

Pete thought that, considering she was the rescuer, this was playing it a little heavy—but he left it to Patsy, edging the convertible around the cars and on toward the studios, certain at least that Carlo could try nothing more with all those police there. Later Pete could worry about the publicity. Now he had Janet to think about. And, watching her legs as she slid over the back of the seat and settled beside him, she was something very nice to worry about—nice, but highly explosive at the moment.

# 17

"And now you say you were there twice." Pete dragged his feet off his desk and stared at Janet.

"But he was alive the first time. I just stopped there on the way to get dressed—for the première." Janet sat wide-eyed on the couch in Pete's office, staring at Pete. She leaned forward earnestly. "He was alive and waiting for some people. He almost rushed me out. But he promised to be ready to go to the première by nine."

"Did he say who?" As the girl shook her head Pete looked at his hands angrily gripping the edge of his desk. "Of course not. Was he frightened? Excited?"

Janet looked thoughtful, then mildly surprised at Pete's guess. "Why, excited. Like a kid getting ready for the circus, only it was a sort of malicious excitement. He said something like, 'This is where Edgar Derwent steps out of the picture,' and then laughed and said, 'That's pretty good, only you don't know it.' Something like that."

"It was very good, only he didn't know it. Derwent stepped out of the picture all right—permanently." Pete rubbed his hair into a snarl and glared at the girl. "I don't know why I keep believing you—but I do. Maybe because it checks. There was a call from one of the airlines about his reservations. Wait a minute!" Pete rumpled his hair forward and then pushed it back almost into place. "The cop said that was a second call. The other one was earlier." He caught up the phone and got the airline reservations. He asked about Derwent's reservations, and made pencil notes on the face of some author's precious script. "Yeah . . . I'm sorry. You must be fed up with the police checking like this. Thank you. You've been very co-operative. Whew!" He hung up and looked at his notations. "Derwent made his reservation two days ago—an urgent. And they called at eight-twenty to tell him there was a stand-by reservation. And again at around two in the morning to confirm a seat. A cancellation. Apparently he was alive at eight-twenty. At least a man answered the phone, and accepted the stand-by. It was Derwent—or some other man. Not you. I've listened to your voice. It's a woman's voice."

"Thanks." Janet smiled gravely. "Are you saying politely it's got sex appeal?" Then an impish grin twinkled through. "And I know all about the bees and the flowers, too."

"Then why do I keep treating you as if you might break or faint or . . ." Pete stared at her. "Maybe Jake's right. You've got that something. Only you're not worth a dime with a murder rap hanging on you. You're distinctly a liability. You're a hot potato!"

"She's not—and you're a brute." Patsy flounced through the door and flopped down beside Janet, her arms around her. "You poor darling. Here, use my shoulder."

Janet's face quivered. All the calmness was swept away by sudden tears, and she buried her face on Patsy's shoulder. The little waitress glared at Pete, and then up at Brady, looming uncertainly in the doorway. She switched back to Pete.

"Why don't you find the murderer and clear this whole thing up. You certainly know a lot about it."

Pete waved his hand wearily. "But not enough. Look, Patsy, the police have facilities I don't have. Hundreds of men to track down clues and witnesses. Laboratory experts. Fingerprint men. Ballistics experts. Oh, I swear at Fels—and he does get my goat. But don't forget, on the whole the police are smart—plenty smart. And they've got organization. They'll find the killer. My job is to keep 'em away from Janet until they do. Only how do I do it? Every paper in the country has her picture."

Brady's Stetson twirled suddenly. "I remember in one of my pictures, I was a bank robber. It was a mistake, but everybody thought I was a bank robber, and they had my picture out, so I wore a beard." Brady hesitated, his honest blue eyes on Janet doubtfully. "Only she'd look kinda funny in a beard."

Janet giggled. "I could join a circus."

"That's it." Pete was on his feet. He pointed at Janet. "Stand up. Over there. Walk. Turn around." He cocked his head, studying her.

Janet pirouetted slowly, looking gravely amused.

Pete glanced at Patsy. "How do you widen hips?"

"I never had that problem. Mine's always been . . ."

"A dirndl." Janet bunched out her trim suit on either hip, showing very nice knees. "They make a girl look hippy."

Pete was nodding to himself. "And a peasant blouse with . . ." He measured chestily in front of himself. "I think that'll do it." He scowled. "Of course you're a blonde."

"And it's natural." Patsy nodded emphatically.

Pete answered the question in Janet's eyes. "The Purloined Letter. Hide something in the most obvious place. And what is there most of in Hollywood—at least most prominent to the eye? Movie actresses. Stick Janet among a flock of 'em and—bingo—she vanishes. And certainly that's the last place Fels would look."

Janet was nodding slowly, as if she had followed Pete's ideas and were just a little ahead of them. "Hair dye. Black. Just as opposite as possible. Dark make-up. Gaudy colors."

Pete turned Janet slowly, lifting her soft, silky hair. "The dye will make it look coarser." And together they began to go over Janet, point by point—eyes, nose, mouth—heavy lipstick splashily applied. Clothes. Violent colors. Teetering heels and platform soles to change her height.

Somehow, before anybody quite knew how it had happened, Pete had got keys from Jorgman, the permanently disillusioned night-watchman who told them that midnight was a funny time to make a screen test but all movie people were crazy. Then Pete had the wardrobe room open and Janet smuggled inside.

While Janet and Patsy withdrew to one of the dressing cubicles Pete explained things to Brady in simple terms. . . . "And we'll fly to Yuma, put the girls on a regular plane for Hollywood, and have a reception for 'em when they get here."

"But, Pete, they're already here. Ain't it simpler to just have a . . ."

"That," stated Pete positively, "is not the way to do it in Hollywood. It's the illusion that counts."

And then Janet stepped out of the dressing cubicle and Pete forgot Brady. She was lovely. She was exotic—Hollywood exotic. Blue-black hair, still damp with dye, swept serenely and sleekly down from a center part and just revealed the tips of her ears, where two gold crescents swung gently against her neck. The softly gathered blouse was low—deeply low and revealing. It slid off one shoulder provocatively. Pete inspected the swishing, gaudily patterned skirt with great intentness, and let his eyes wander down the slim legs, now in sheer black stockings, to feet in vivid green wedgies studded with gold-headed nails. He gulped uneasily.

"You'll do. But can't you . . ." He made an unhappy, uneasy motion as if he were hitching up his suspenders.

Janet fluttered the long eyelashes. "And step out of character?" The bare shoulder flickered and the blouse trembled on the verge of complete revelation. "Don't worry. There's adhesive tape underneath." And then she laughed, her head thrown back, showing the long, lovely line of her throat. Her fingers snapped, and the wedgies beat a quick clacking tattoo. She lowered her head and looked at Pete from under the long fringe of lashes, suddenly sputtering Spanish.

Brady, blinking at the changeling, suddenly laughed and spat back at her, his drawl suddenly lost in the quick staccato Spanish, and they laughed together.

"Hey!" Pete stared at his prize Western star. "You can speak Spanish?" And then at Janet. "And you?"

"McQueeney, Texas, is practically in Mexico."

"And you, Tom. You never told anybody. Where'd you learn Spanish?"

"I'm from Texas, too. Ain't anybody asked me. . . ."

"And we've been dubbing in our Spanish releases! Okay." He held out his hand to Janet, turning her slowly, approvingly. . . . "We'll get moving. You certainly did a bang-up job."

"Hey." Patsy stuck her head out of the cubicle. "Don't I get any of the credit?"

Pete felt giddily relieved. This was going to work.

He felt sure of that now. "Credit, Patsy? You get cash! As of now, you're hired. As personal manager of . . . let's see . . . of *Señorita* Carmen Merita! How's that?"

"In that case," Patsy stalked out of the cubicle, peering into her purse, "as manager of *Señorita* Carmen Merita, we want some salary . . . cash salary." She held open the purse. It was practically empty. At least, Pete couldn't see any money among the strictly feminine debris. "Or do you think little girls live on love?"

Pete squeezed Patsy's arm gratefully. "My experience has been that lots of little girls live very well on love. But you'll get cash, plenty of it. Only right now, I've got a plane waiting. Ted Mason, our stunt man, has his Howard warming up at the airport. He'll fly us to Yuma. . . ." He was already urging them toward the door.

Now his only job was to sell his new Mexican actress to Jake.

# 18

After what was practically a triumphal ride from the airport to the hotel, Pete finally succeeded in getting the photographers and reporters out of Carmen Merita's suite by the always expeditious method of telling them free drinks were being served in Private Dining Room #6, which Loeb Studios maintained for just such emergencies. Pete waved the last and somewhat reluctant cameraman out—he insisted he had ulcers but there was nothing wrong with his eyesight, and he frankly preferred Carmen to Carstairs—and turned back to see Jake Tobias mopping the top of his bald head with an immense and immaculate handkerchief.

From under the shelter of the handkerchief, Jake looked from Pete to Carmen and back. "With my blood pressure up to two hundred, I should sell out! Pete, where do you find her?" He shook the handkerchief at Janet.

Pete attempted an airy wave of the hand. "I told you. Down in Mexico."

"So you tell reporters down in Mexico. Think you can maybe fool Papa Jake so easy? Max Factor makeup I know like the back of my hand. That costume is strictly from stock. I use it last in 'Mexican Sleighride.'"

Pete deflated onto what, for some reason, was called a love-seat. "If you spotted her, Jake, those reporters . . ."

"Reporters!" Jake snorted indignantly. "They ain't spent ten-fifteen hours looking at pictures of her. But me, Pete, I know every move of the hands, the tilt of the head, the shape of the ears . . ." As Janet gasped, the little producer turned on her almost fiercely. "Yes, and the shape of the legs. I ain't so old I shouldn't notice legs." Jake thought that over for a moment. "In the line of business strictly."

Pete flapped his hands. "I had to do something, Jake; hide her somewhere. So I thought of 'The Purloined Letter'. . ."

"Oi! So now you rob the United States mail! Pete, can't you do anything simple—like maybe a little breaking and entering?"

"We tried that last night." Patsy subsided on a lounge beside Tom Brady, who still looked as if he were waiting for the old mine shaft to collapse or the time bomb to go off in the sixth reel so he could gallop in to the rescue. "And it worked, too." Patsy twinkled at Jake complacently.

"And what did you steal that time?"

"Me. . . ." Janet pushed herself up from the arm of the sofa on which she had been posing and came to stand contritely before him. "I've caused everybody a lot of grief. I'm being a nuisance. I think I'd better call the district attorney and give myself up. . . ."

"Look!" Jake grabbed her arm, shaking one plump pink sausage of a finger under her nose. "On that face . . ." He stared at Janet's heavily rouged lips and mascaraed eyes and shuddered. "Maybe not on that hussy's face you paint over it, but on the face underneath, Papa Jake has seen the truth. You don't kill anybody—even a heel like Derwent. But does Bynum Fels know that? Can he see truth in a face? No. Maybe, after he gets you, it looks like an easy case, so he don't look further. But now he's got to look. And when he looks hard enough, he'll find out who done it." He whirled on Pete. "Who did done it?" He flapped his arms. "Who robbed the United States mail? Who broke and entered what? Why don't somebody tell Papa Jake something?"

Pete got up and pushed the little man back into a chair, then straddled the back of another and faced him. "Here's the story to date." And to an accompaniment of clucks and vague, disapproving murmurs, Jake listened and mopped his bald head.

"Get that murderer, Pete, so there shouldn't be more murders." He sighed wearily. "I gotta go now." He glared around at the fake Carmen. "And put that hussy somewhere I can't see her. Such a ruination for a nice girl turns me sick to my stomach."

"I'll send 'em out to Brady's ranch."

Pete bundled Brady, Patsy and Janet into a studio car, and then accompanied Jake back to the studio—where new grief awaited them, in a telegram.

Jake read it three times before he groaned and threw the paperweight through the glass door panel. Pete picked up the telegram and read it.

> *"Cancelled tour. Am returning. Janet my favorite person. Don't let anything happen to her or I'll go to King Brothers.*
>
> *Robert Emery"*

"Always he threatens to go to King Brothers. Quickies! Why couldn't once maybe he threaten to go to RKO?" But Jake's usual force was missing and there was even a twinkle in his eye—a suspiciously moist twinkle. "Pete, he believes in her, too."

Emily Fishbein's trout-like face appeared, and her hand held out a second telegram.

Jake read it and pushed it across the desk, as if he were afraid it might contaminate him.

"Amelia! She's coming out. On a plane. From her coffin even she would get up if it makes trouble for Jake. And like getting up from a coffin it is, Pete. For three years I ain't had trouble from Amelia because she's in bed grieving for the no-good son of hers. Now comes this. Earthquakes I take easy—with just maybe a coupla aspirins. But Amelia!"

So the fabulous Amelia Alwyn was coming to Hollywood.

"She's had tough luck with that boy of hers, hasn't she?"

"On him birth control should be made retroactive. Such a little stinker he is—was. Kidnapping!"

"Who did he kidnap? Did her money get him off?"

"He got kidnapped. Gone four-five days, and poor Amelia scared into conniption fits. She got ransom notes."

"Did she pay the ransom? I mean, is that how he got back?"

"Half a million. After that no-good comes back, does he co-operate with the cops or the F.B.I.? Not him. And Amelia clams up, also. And says she's scared they'll try again. She was glad to get him back. Personally I would be glad, whoever takes him should keep him."

"Any explanation? From him, I mean?"

"I should know about it? That boy is one thing Amelia don't talk much about. But she threatens to cut him out of her will, I know, because he runs away. Four, maybe five years ago. Three years ago he is killed."

"In the war?"

"Him? In a war? He ran away and hid in Mexico—and somebody knifed him. Girl, most likely. Only Amelia won't admit he's dead."

"Then that was what Phillips was talking about—Amelia's whim . . ."

"And don't forget Amelia's got a whim of iron." Jake groaned. "And she's coming here."

"That man's here again." Pete nodded at his unhappy boss and walked out, avoiding the assistant district attorney. But he couldn't avoid the bulk of Russell in the doorway. The beefy detective put a huge hand on Pete's chest and shoved. Pete stumbled back into the room, pivoted and caught himself, hands on the edge of the desk. For a moment he felt a hot surge of anger, and then he grinned at Fels. "And who is going to act as bodyguard for the bodyguard—on dark nights?"

"He's managed to live this long."

"I've heard fate is kind to fools and drunkards." Pete glanced at Russell doubtfully. "Do you drink?"

"I ain't no drunkard," Russell roared, "if that's what you're getting at."

"I don't think that was what Mister Hack had in mind, Russell." And Fels' mouth twitched slightly under his oddly rugged mustache.

Mollified, Russell slumped against the door frame. "'Ain't nobody leavin'."

Jake eyed the door and Russell's bulk as if he had thought highly of the idea of leaving but given it up. He sank down behind his desk and shoved some prints of Derwent toward Fels. "The stills you asked for."

"Russell's a little enthusiastic. I'm not detaining anyone." Fels turned to Pete. "I haven't forgotten you got my one witness released—and she got killed."

"Oh, I did that."

Fels grunted as if he'd been struck, and they all whirled to face the door, where Alwyn Phillips was peering distastefully across Russell's lounging bulk. He looked up and saw them staring at him.

"Shouldn't I have? Pete said if we got her free she could give us a lead as to who recommended Derwent here—and that was important."

Fels snorted. “Important? So important that somebody shut her mouth—permanently.”

“Oh, dear—and I only wanted to help.”

# 19

Pete stared at the dapper banker. "Why the devil did you use my name? And how did you work it?"

Phillips glanced at Russell and then stepped over his feet, rather like a cat over a puddle. "Why, it was quite simple. I called our legal department and told them to arrange it. In your name, of course, since the costs must be charged to your department."

"How are you going to enter this account? Under 'Murder, Expenses for'?"

"This is not the time to be facetious," Phillips told him frigidly. "Mister Fels, I apologize for my conduct in getting Miss Winters released."

"Apologize to Miss Winters. She's down at the morgue."

Phillips shivered distastefully. "Aren't you being a bit gruesome?"

"That's my business. Being gruesome. Not because I like it, but because people go around making other people into corpses, and I have to look at them. It makes things a little gruesome. So you got Germaine Winters out on bail, at the request of Pete Hack. What did you do with her? Did you pick her up? Send a studio car? Have a lawyer meet her?"

"Oh! The studio lawyer. He posted bond and then phoned me. I told him to send her home in a taxi. I suppose he did."

"He did. We found the taxi. He delivered her home at seven-forty-five. At eight-twenty she was dead. With three bullets from a .22 in her." Fels growled, glanced at Pete. "Did you notify Mister Hack his witness was available?"

Phillips shook his head and wet his lips. "No. I couldn't locate him. I learned later that he was in a bar." Alwyn's eyebrows lifted slightly. "In several bars."

"For once, legitimately—I think. Checking alibis."

Phillips shrugged. "I only did what I considered my duty to the company."

"Even Pete Hack had sense enough to know she was better off locked up." Which, coming from Fels, was very close to a compliment. He turned to Jake. "We'll take a batch of those stills. . . ." And he set about sorting quickly through them handing those he wanted to a very sullen Russell. The rest he left scattered across Jake's massive desk and departed in minor parade formation.

Phillips watched them go and then turned to Jake, who shushed him with a violent, chopping gesture.

"I was just going to ask about. . ."

"Don't. Every time you ask a question it's got a $64 answer." Jake sighed, spotted Amelia's telegram and stiffened. He pointed tragically at it and then stabbed a plump finger at Pete. "Do something."

Pete looked over the telephone hooked between shoulder and ear. "I'm doing it. Your car is out front now. You're due at the airport in thirty minutes."

Jake wiped a shaky hand across his several chins and sighed. Phillips stiffened, his mouth primming into a tiny buttonhole. "Not another actress! Really, Mr. Tobias, the way you . . ."

But Jake was already around his desk and headed for the door. He stared witheringly at the New York banker. "And I thought you give me troubles. Hah!" And Jake stalked out, his head bowed, as if he were marching to the tumbrel and the execution block. Pete followed, giving the startled Phillips a quick pat.

"You can go back and play with your assets and liabilities now. . . ."

Alwyn Phillips looked as if he were about to explain that assets and liabilities were something you didn't play with, so Pete hurried to catch up with Jake.

Knowing Los Angeles traffic and the location of the airport, Pete realized he had a few minutes before he would be needed as greeter to Amelia Alwyn at the hotel. Now he wanted to talk to Bill Katon.

He found him in a cubbyhole of an office glaring in bafflement at a typewriter as if it had just bitten him.

Pete perched on the edge of the nicked and battered desk. "Now look, Bill, I've got a client accused of killing Derwent and I think I've got a right to know something about the guy she's supposed to have killed. That's only fair." Pete shrugged elaborately. "Of course, any confidential stuff . . ." He let that trail off, watching Bill.

"None of it's confidential, except maybe the names of blackmail victims and that stinking material he had. Nobody gets that."

Katon opened a limp, well-thumbed notebook and scowled at it. "This is all we've got on Edgar Derwent."

Pete leaned over Bills massive shoulder and studied the sprawled notes. He eased the book out of Bill's hands and hurriedly whipped through pages of laboriously written notes. Frowning, he closed the book over his finger. "From this, Edgar Derwent might have been born last October."

"So?"

"He was more than eight months old."

Bill grinned. "Maybe he was one o' them juvenile delinquents." He tapped the book. "That's as far back as Edgar Derwent goes. He just turned up. We'll know more about him later. I sent his prints to Washington. And on your tip the F.B.I. wants a quick tie-up with Spigotti, so I figure they'll speed it up. Maybe that'll show us who he was before he got to be Edgar Derwent. Or could be he kept outa trouble till he slipped up the other night."

"Derwent was a pro. Or the next thing to one. He's bound to have a record." Pete glared at the limp book. He opened it, thumbing through the pages. He paused at one. "Pawnshops? Since when does a guy in a money-mill like blackmail need to hock his studs?" He glanced down the list. "Golf clubs. Ring. Watch. Silver frame. Matched leather suitcases. Another. . . . Briefcase." Pete ran his finger down the list.

Bill nodded solemnly. "A lot of it he redeemed. Just last week. The suitcases, briefcase, frame, wrist watch, and one of the rings."

"So he was in the chips again. We know that. I even know where some of the chips came from."

"Don't tell me!" Bill hastily threw up a hand. "I don't want to know you was paying blackmail. I might have to do something about it."

Pete grinned, then nodded and returned to the book, studying the dates this time. "He hocked most of the stuff between October and Christmas. Either he ran out of hockables or he got a new source of money."

"He got a job. With Loeb Films."

Pete shook his head. "Have you any idea what an extra gets? I know what we paid Derwent. I checked. And it wouldn't have paid the rent on the dump he was in." Pete slapped the book back on the desk. "And the stuff wasn't stolen?"

"Not the stuff we saw. Leastwise, we didn't have pick-up orders on any of it. The really good stuff, the kind we might have identified, he redeemed himself, like I told you."

"Well, didn't you get a look at it?"

"Huh? How'd we get a look at . . ." Bill blinked. "I'll be a monkey's uncle! Hello, nephew!" He was around the desk, thrusting Pete aside and down the hall before Pete could regain his balance. He spun heavily against the edge of the desk and decided to remain there. It wouldn't take Bill long to find out.

It didn't. In a few minutes Bill was back, staring at Pete. "It wasn't there. Suitcase, briefcase, everything. Gone."

"He could have sent it ahead to the airport." Pete frowned over this. "No, he didn't know he had a reservation before he was killed. So the killer took it. He must have!"

"This Janet West is a she. You got your tenses mixed."

"Gender. And I didn't get 'em mixed. Look, Bill. Your own witness saw this Janet West leaving Derwent's bungalow. Right?" At Bill's nod, he went on. "That's the only thing he's got on Janet West, isn't it?"

"What more do you want? Photographs? Ain't a witness enough?"

"And what did the witness see?" He tapped the book. "It's in there. Read it."

"I don't need to. She seen this West babe sneaking out the back door of Derwent's cottage with a gun in one hand and a big, floppy purse in the other."

Bill's mouth kept going but no words came. He looked at his two scoop-shovel hands perplexedly.

"And on top of her head she was balancing two matched leather suitcases, a brief case and assorted jewelry."

"Bro-ther!" Bill whistled softly. "Fels ain't gonna like this."

"But I do. Oh, brother, I do."

"Hey! Pete! You didn't get that from me, you know."

"You're damn right I didn't, Bill. You just focused it for me. Every scrap of that—except the hockshop deal—was in the papers. Even photographs of Derwent's place—and no luggage. Fels has been running off at the mouth. Now I'm going to pack all those words in a nice set of matched leather luggage and make him eat 'em! Luggage and all."

Pete started back for the hotel, strangely lighthearted. Janet couldn't be guilty—and he had figured it out.

# 20

Patsy opened the door a crack, one belligerent eye glaring through at Pete. Then the door was flung open and she stepped back, lowering the heavy vase. "Wolves! Give me travelling salesmen any day to Hollywood reporters." She grinned at him.

Janet lounged in the doorway to the bedroom, her newly darkened hair tousled and magically swirled into a gorgeous frame for her oval face. The heavily mascaraed eyes dropped, then came up, blazing at him. "Ah, *señor!* You are so . . ." Her hands butterflied a pantomime of ecstasy and the peasant blouse trembled. She was heart-stoppingly lovely and as Spanish as a night in Madrid.

Pete tried to keep it impersonal, even in his thinking. Yup, he told himself, the kid's an actress. Jake can really spot 'em. From a newsreel shot that didn't run thirty seconds, Jake had picked a winner. He winked at Janet. "Break it up, kid. The camera boys have gone. This is Uncle Pete."

Janet held her pose in the doorway a moment longer, eyeing him from under the dark, beaded lashes; then she sighed and stepped into the room, walking firmly and rather primly. She made straight for a cigarette box and fumbled with it. Finally she smiled up at him. "I thought I ought to stay in character."

"Sure. But just don't melt my backbone with it." Pete held out a light and she cupped her hand around his, holding the match steady. Until then he hadn't realized it was wobbly. He drew his hand back, snapping out the match. "Where was Derwent's luggage?" He made it brusque.

Janet drew back, cigarette held very still. "Luggage? Oh! Matching cowhide. Reddish. Two suitcases. They were by his desk. I remember. That was the first time I was there." She shut her eyes briefly, shook her head. "I don't see them. Just him—and those pictures scattered all over. And the gun." She shivered slightly.

"That'll clear you." He told her about Germaine's testimony, the only evidence Fels had against her. "I can't point it out. It would made Fels suspicious. But he'll wake up to it soon." Pete grinned. "In fact, I've already wound the clock and set the alarm."

"And I've still got to wear all this gook and be Carmen Merita?"

"For a while, kid. It's safer."

"Safer?" Janet said it just as there was a knock at the door. Pete was faintly aware that Patsy had caught up her vase again and was advancing on the door. He was also aware that Janet was regarding him oddly. "So you think it's safer?" She nodded crisply. "In that case . . ." She swished around in front of him, one shoulder wriggling out of the peasant blouse, her eyes slitted and dark. "We have company. So I be Carmen. I give a performance!" Her eyes opened wide, blazing.

"You . . ." She launched into a shrieking crescendo of Spanish, pounded at him with her fists, the sudden violence of her attack forcing him back. His heel caught on the clawfoot of a chair and he lost his balance, flailing wildly. He grabbed at Janet-Carmen's rounded, golden-cream shoulder, and she shrieked wildly.

Just before they pitched over in a wild flailing of arms and legs, Pete saw Patsy fling the door open and then rush toward them, vase upraised in both hands. He ducked, trying to roll his head into comparative safety under the chair. The vase crashed on the arm, bits and pieces showering stingingly down across his cheek.

"Stop! This instant!" The voice was pitched to carry and to command. One he recognized of old.

Carmens pummeling stopped abruptly and he felt her weight slowly lift. Peering from under the chair, he could see Carmen's ridiculously high-heeled platform shoes, twinkling with stones, gaudy with color. And near them Patsy's plain, sensible shoes. He didn't want to look any further.

"And come out from under that chair! Unless, of course, you've lost a collar button."

Pete scrambled out and sat up, trying to grin at the pair just inside the doorway. "Hi!" He got up lankily. "We were just . . ." Before the stern, appraising eyes of the tiny, austere little woman beside Jake, Pete felt his words drying up.

"He eeensolt Carmen!" Janet-Carmen stamped her foot, listened to it, found it good and stomped both of them in rapid succession.

"Behave yourself." Amelia Alwyn whisked across the room, her long skirts hiding any motion of the tiny feet underneath.

She glared at Janet-Carmen. "How did he insult you? Did he try to kiss you?"

"No, *señora.*" Janet-Carmen fluttered her hands. . . . "That ees exoctly eet. He didn't try to kiss me."

"Oh!" Amelia whisked herself around with her odd mechanical doll motion and plunked down into a chair, her skirts hiking only enough to show the tips of tiny shoes.

She reared back her head and peered at Pete. "You are a cad!" She glinted belligerently at Patsy. "I suppose you were breaking up the pottery because he wouldn't kiss you, too."

Patsy planted both feet firmly in front of Amelia, hands on her hips. "When I can't get a man to kiss me without cracking crockery over him, that'll be the day there's an earthquake in Ireland, with all the Muldoons turning in their graves simultaneous."

Amelia looked imperiously at Jake. "You might at least introduce us."

"Oh! Me!" Jake pressed a hand on either side of his head and rocked it. "Schlemiel! Amelia Alwyn, Carmen Merita. Her secretary, Patsy Muldoon. . . . Now everybody knows everybody let's sit down." Jake let himself down into one of the hotel's deeper chairs, getting almost lost in its depths, his eyes on Janet-Carmen.

Janet-Carmen shook one of the delicate, mittened hands with grave courtesy, and Amelia twinkled. "I admired your performance." Pete had an idea they hadn't fooled this bright-eyed old lady, but he had no time for further speculation. There was a crisp knock at the door. Patsy glanced at Pete for orders and then went to open it.

Alwyn Phillips pushed it sharply back and strode in, his precise and meticulous anger aimed directly at Jake. "You should have told me Aunt Amelia was arriving!" He whipped across the room, scissoring his long legs in quick, jerky strides. "My dear Aunt Amelia! You can't know how delighted I am to see you. Had I known you were arriving, I should most certainly have been at the airport to meet you." He reached down and caught up one of the tiny hands, sandwiching it between his and patting and molding it as if he were going to make it into a hoecake. "I'm delighted to see you." He smiled toothily.

Amelia tugged her hand away. "I doubt that, Alwyn. You're probably worried silly wondering if I'm going to take the studio away from you." Alwyn Phillips sucked in his breath sharply for a quick "No," but didn't get a chance to use it. Amelia plowed right on. "Perhaps I shall. Scandalous things have been happening since you took over."

Phillips began to protest but Amelia cut him short. "Oh, sit down, Alwyn, if you intend to stay. And for heaven's sake, relax! You're as jittery as an old maid at a burglars' convention. Flirt with the girls, if you know how. Jake and I want to reminisce. When you get to be my age, old times always seem better than the present—and probably much better than they actually were." She turned to catch Janet-Carmen frowning at her. Very delicately Amelia put one tiny hand to her hat and then to the orchid Pete had sent to the plane. "Is something wrong with me, child?"

Janet-Carmen flushed, smiling uncertainly. "Oh, your pardon, *señora*. No. It is just . . . I have seen you somewhere before."

Amelia laughed. "Not unless you've been in West Long Branch, New Jersey, lately. I haven't left it for ten years, isn't it, Alwyn?"

Phillips jerked his eyes away from the girl to blink at his aunt. "Oh. Nine years, seven months. You attended Uncle Wilmot's funeral on . . ."

Amelia ignored the rest of it, smiling at the girl. "I shall never need a diary as long as Alwyn's memory holds out."

"Then your peeekchair. In a newspaper, perhaps? Aftair all, you are a famous person."

Amelia shook her head, "Not even as a girl. My father, Commodore Whortle, was afraid of kidnapers, so none of us children were allowed to be photographed. And now that it no longer matters, I find being un-photographed a pleasant eccentricity. It also saves me a great deal of time."

"But, Amelia," Jake tented his fat fingers over his round little stomach, "you were photographed."

Amelia looked faintly puzzled, a small frown forming, then fading to a smile. "Oh—that. Just for the family, Jake. Oh—and those horrible things you have made for passports. But," she smiled at the girl, "I hardly think you saw my passport. It's just that I look like every old lady of seventy."

Janet-Carmen accepted that with a gracious little nod, and turned to answer something Alwyn Phillips said.

"I see." He shifted uneasily in his chair, apparently fearful of interrupting something Jake and Amelia were saying, yet anxious to speak. Finally he stood up, drawing their attention. He tilted his chin aggressively, prissing his mouth. "Perhaps the others can stay away from their jobs, but I feel that mine claims all my attention."

"So?" Jake lifted mild eyes to him. "For now, Amelia is my job. Carmen is Pete's. We stay."

"Oh, run along, Alwyn." Amelia waved him away in exasperation. "But you should let that banker's conscience of yours off the leash sometimes. 'Bye."

Phillips made a formal tour of farewells and then practically scuttled for the door, beating Pete to it by a whisker. Then he was through it and gone. Pete went back and sat down beside Janet-Carmen with a sigh. He stretched his long legs, leaning back in his chair and practicing a leer on Janet-Carmen. She stuck her tongue out at him.

"Mexican!" Amelia said it so sharply Pete jerked upright, staring at her. "Just about as Mexican as my mother's apple pies!" She whirled on Jake, holding up a tiny mittened hand. "I don't want to know who she is. I have an idea it's all slightly illegal and I'm better off not knowing. After all, I do have the remnants of a Puritan conscience and I just might tell the authorities." She smiled a crumpled-rose smile at Pete. "But I can't if I don't know anything."

Janet-Carmen inspected herself all over, even turning her hands slowly in front of her. "Where did I slip up?"

"Oh, if you'd been a cantina girl, you'd have scratched instead of punching Pete. And you smoothed down your skirts when you were fighting."

"My modesty!" Janet-Carmen laughed a very hearty Janet laugh. Then she sobered. "But you mustn't blame Pete. I'm a cover-up, all right, but not for anything Pete did wrong." She sat forward, hands clasped, thrust down between her knees like a very small, very earnest little girl. "He has been simply wonderful about . . ."

Amelia twinkled at her. "I'm sure he has. And I rarely blame people without getting facts first." She looked around at them mildly, "But once I get the facts—I generally do something." There was steel beneath the rose petals.

Jake shut his eyes and shivered. "Mostly drastic, with trimmings. Once she shot me. But only slightly."

"I could do it again." And from somewhere among the Edwardian ruffles and furbelows Amelia Alwyn had produced a tiny gun, her eyes still gay, but the tiny mittened hand rock-steady.

Jake looked at the gun, shrugging. "I tell her to shoot. If she kills me, she never gets her money back. Also, I don't got to worry about it further. Her money is worrying me to an early grave." He sighed. "Now a tailor shop . . ."

The girls blinked as the gun disappeared as mysteriously as it had appeared. Amelia smiled up at them. "When you have as much money as I do, you sometimes need protection." She stood up, a diminutive figure of command. "I'm tired. Take me to my room, Jake. You, too,

Pete." At the door she smiled back at the girls, singling out Janet-Carmen. "I trust Jake. But as for Pete . . ." She shrugged delicately, almost primly. "I've rather lost faith in a man who has to be bludgeoned into a kiss—especially when the girl's as pretty as you. He's probably a cad, and you're well rid of him."

# 21

Pete went over Janet's story with her again, from the first letter Edgar Derwent had written, through her various meetings with him, to the last two visits to his bungalow. Nothing emerged, except the incongruity of Derwent acting for Robert Emery. That made no sense. Emery hated and despised the man. Surely he wouldn't have empowered such a man to act as his emissary with Janet, his favorite. Remembering some of the pictures in Derwent's rooms, Pete shuddered. No, not even under the threat of blackmail would Emery have put Janet in Derwent's hands. But—it was an inspiration and Pete decided to test it. He thumbed through his address book, found the number and called.

A woman's voice answered, alert, vigorous. Was she Naomi Talbot, Robert Emery's secretary? She was. Had Edgar Derwent been a regular visitor? The voice was less vigorous, guarded. Not regular, no. He had called once or twice. An insolent, highhanded man. Had he ever—and Pete crossed his fingers on this one—had an opportunity to go through Emery's mail? The voice was surprised. How had Pete guessed? She had gone to tell Robert that Derwent was in the den and come back to find him perched on the edge of the desk insolently reading Robert's mail. She had told Robert and he had ordered Derwent out, never to come back. He had gone. Was there anything else? Yes, when would Robert return? She was expecting him tomorrow. He'd missed a plane connection and was coming on by train. The Super Chief. There was a new warmth when she said that, and Pete hung up, suspecting the spinsterish secretary was in love with her boss. He was also satisfied he had the answer to how Derwent got hold of Janet's letter and pictures. With Emery leaving for location takes, he would have a clear field with a lovely girl. It sounded like Derwent. That it hadn't worked out to be as simple as Derwent had undoubtedly anticipated was due entirely to Janet. Pete grinned at her. "Now we know." He glanced at Patsy who was cautiously opening the door.

It was thrust rudely back, throwing Patsy off balance, and Carlo Spigotti walked in, his dark face still and cold. He waved one hand in an abrupt gesture. "Take it easy."

Pete sat perfectly still, watching. He didn't have a gun and he suspected the dapper little man had a shoulder holster under the padding of his double-breasted suit. Janet barely turned in her chair, looked at him, shrugged and reached for a cigarette.

"Who ees theees mon?"

"A minor piece of garbage." Pete lit Janet-Carmen's cigarette, with one eye on Patsy, who looked murderous and tempestuous.

Carlo jerked a thumb at her without taking his eyes off Janet-Carmen. "Tell the babe to keep still. This is a friendly visit." To prove it the little racketeer split his dark face in a thin, narrow smile. "I ain't even preferring charges. Breaking up my cocktail lounge. I'm even forgetting that crack you just made."

"Nice of you." Pete helped himself to a cigarette and lit it. "It would be kind of tough if you pressed charges—and found yourself facing a kidnap and assault rap, wouldn't it?"

Carlo shrugged. "So we sit out this dance."

"It was a fool move, Carlo, kidnapping Janet."

"You're making me cry." Carlo settled himself on the arm of a chair, his dark head weaving slightly to keep them all in view. As yet he had made no move toward the gun.

Janet-Carmen sat very still, only her hand with the cigarette moving. Even Patsy had backed against the wall and was quiet. Pete considered possibilities of tackling Carlo and discarded them. Somebody could get shot before he made it. He sucked on the cigarette thoughtfully.

"Not that I think you're too bright, Spigotti, but why put yourself on a spot that way? You didn't need Janet . . ." Then it dawned. "But you did need what you thought she had. The suitcases. You knew they hadn't been found, or the newspapers . . ." He squinted at the curl of smoke. The idea was tenuous yet, as unsubstantial as the smoke. "There was evidence in those suitcases that the cops would have acted on. And they didn't. And the newspapers . . ."

"You're three laps behind, wise guy." But under the sneer Carlo was nervously surprised, like a man who has underrated his opponent. "I needed some clean hankies." He chuckled nervously at that. "'Cause I'm keeping my nose clean, see?" He started slowly for the door, in a crab-wise saunter that kept them all in view. "Well, so long." He grinned crookedly. "I got what I came for."

"It couldn't have been much." Pete tried to shrug it away.

"I dunno. Maybe it wasn't much I come for. Just a look at the doll." He jerked his head at Janet-Carmen. "She turned up so neat, I just had to figure."

Pete managed to look surprised, or hoped he did. "You mean Carmen Merita? Don't be nuts, Spigotti."

Carlo sneered. "So the hair's dyed, the face is painted. Okay. Me, I see millions of faces. I ain't interested. But gams, they're different. I notice them." He sniggered. "And I had a nice look at Janet's. And them cheesecake pictures of the new tamale from Mexico." He blew a leering kiss at Janet-Carmen. "And me, I know you got Janet West. The cops don't. So I can figure." He put out a hand for the doorknob just as the phone rang. He froze, watching them.

Pete reached slowly for the phone, his eyes on Spigotti. "They know we're here. If we don't answer, somebody might investigate."

Carlo hesitated, his hand hovering at his lapel. "Okay, answer it. But no tip-offs or I might have to get fancy with the doll." The gun was out now and Carlo sidled around the room to the bedroom door, reaching in with his free hand. "I'll just listen in, in case you try any tricks, like double talking. I know your cop friends."

Pete nodded and picked up the phone. It was Katon reporting on Derwent's fingerprints, as promised. "You loafer, sitting around in hotel suites while the police work their butts to the bone."

Pete grinned across the phone at Carlo. "Not yours; it's too well padded. What's the scoop?"

"They've tied him up to the Fred Alwyn snatch. His prints match a latent on the ransom demand. First break in that case in five years, and the guy's dead!" Katon sounded aggrieved. "And five hundred grand still missing. Maybe it's in them missing suitcases."

"Could be."

"Well . . ." Bill said it as if he had expected more reaction. "You ain't talkative."

"I've got company."

"Oh!" Bill sighed. "Okay. Back to the grind. Be seeing yuh, kid."

Pete hung up, watching Carlo in the doorway. The conversation had certainly changed him. He strolled out confidently, gun tucked away. He even grinned crookedly at Pete, waved flippantly at Janet-Carmen and Patsy, and strolled toward the door, looking pleased. "Now I know how the score adds up. Thanks." He pointed a skinny, slightly crooked finger. "Don't think about tipping anybody off I'm on the way down. If anybody stops me, I'm givin' 'em an earful about an eyeful." He aimed the finger at Janet-Carmen and opened the door. He slithered through, grinning around the edge of the door at them. "I gotta see somebody or I wouldn'ta run like this." He laughed as he pulled the door closed and went off down the hall, whistling a tune faintly recognizable as "I'm Sitting on Top of the World."

# 22

Pete set out for Corliss Petry's place. It was a small, neat, and astonishingly modern apartment for the gentle, almost motherly Corliss to have.

Her eyes went bleak when Pete asked her about her son. "That's over, Pete. Finished. And much of my life with it. I just want to forget it. Please."

"But can you?"

"That's cruel!" Corliss turned away from him, leaning her head against the soft dove-gray cushions. "I want to. I'm trying to."

"How do you know Derwent was responsible for your son's death?" He reminded her that she had said it.

"Oh, I knew him then. And he was with Davey at Tia Juana. After they sent me Davey's body, I went down. To investigate. I just couldn't believe Davey would commit suicide." She crammed the knuckles of one hand against her mouth. "I still can't. Davey loved living."

"What did you find out?"

Corliss stared back along the bleak road to the past. Slowly she shook her head. "Nothing. In a place like Spigotti's . . ."

"Spigotti's! Carlo Spigotti?"

"Yes. A sort of cantina. A dance hall."

Pete nodded. "I know the sort of place Spigotti would run."

"It was a blank. Davey hadn't been using his real name down there, so the authorities couldn't help me even if they had wanted to. And I don't think these wanted to. Death seemed commonplace to them, I think. And suicides were just a shrug. There were at least two others during the week I was there. One of them just a girl."

"And Derwent was there?"

"But not as Derwent. Andrews, I think he called himself then. I hated him even then. He was so sly. He oozed around."

"And when you learned he was back in Hollywood you threatened to kill him."

Corliss smiled faintly. "Threatened to. If he didn't leave town."

"Do you think you actually frightened him?"

Corliss shrugged. "He was leaving town when he was killed." She sat back with a sigh. "I think whoever did it deserves a medal."

"For Derwent, yes—but what about Virginia Struthers? And Germaine? A medal for each?"

Corliss gasped. "No! Oh, Pete, I don't know how to think any more. Of course not. The murderer must be caught." She looked at him for a long moment. "Are you going to catch the killer?"

Pete grinned ruefully. "I might have to try. I'm no Johnny Liddel or Perry Mason. Now Carlo thinks he is. He's got it all figured out. At least he hints he has. I don't know."

"Carlo? Carlo Spigotti? Little, dark, swaggering man? Over-neat?"

"Sounds about like him. Why?"

Corliss was again looking off down a lonesome road. "He was one of them that killed Davey." She stood up and moved slowly toward the big front window. Standing to one side, she peered out furtively and then turned back to Pete with a frown. "He isn't there now."

Pete leapt to the window, peering out. The street was not deserted but neither was it overcrowded. He couldn't make out any figure as Carlo's, however. He swung back into the room. "Carlo was here?" He pointed out and down.

Corliss nodded. "He followed me. From the studio. I saw him hanging around there. That's why I accepted a ride with Charles."

"Charles Abbott? But you and he . . ."

"Oh, we don't actually fight, Pete." She smiled ruefully. "And I don't think he liked it. He was polishing apples. Taking the Big Wheel home. I think Charles wanted a cozy twosome, but he couldn't refuse. And Phillips didn't mind riding with the hired help. It was free." She lifted her delicate eyebrows. "Are all bankers tightwads?"

"I never got close enough to 'em to study their habits. And if Phillips is a sample, I don't want to."

He peered out the window again and then came back to sit down. "So Carlo followed you home?"

"I didn't actually see him following—but he was across the street when I drew the shades. Marilyn was mixing the drinks so . . ."

"Marilyn? Aren't you getting a bit chummy in odd places?"

"Oh, she hitched onto the party at the studio." Corliss grinned for the first time. "She was trying to make time with Phillips, only he didn't know it. Can a man really be that blind? Charles was practically sulking by the time we stopped off here for drinks. It was a charming party. The Marx Brothers couldn't have raised a laugh among us."

"How long ago was this?"

Corliss glanced at a tiny French clock. "They cleared out half an hour ago."

"Together?"

"They only had Charles' car. That's why he was so furious with Marilyn. He had to drive all the way out to her place. Up Canyon Drive. That meant he didn't have that all-important private conference with Phillips. He had to drop him and take Marilyn."

"Did you see Carlo after they left?"

Corliss thought for a moment. "I didn't notice. I went right in to a shower. And then you came."

"Why would Carlo follow you?" He tried that question with variations but Corliss had no answers. Or wasn't giving any. Finally he left, baffled.

He swung his car into the curb by Abbott's place and got out, keeping an eye out for Carlo but not seeing him. Both the doorman and the switchboard operator assured him Charles Abbott had not come in as yet. Their supercilious attitudes also suggested that Mister Abbott would not be likely to be at home to such as Pete when he was in. The garage attendant was less haughty but no more informative. Mister Abbott's car was not in and hadn't been in since morning.

He drove on out past the homes of famous and once-famous stars, on up through the hills to the more modern places with ranch-type houses oddly jammed on to barely levelled spots, and up to Marilyn Courtney's "Court Hall."

He found Marilyn lounging at the edge of her swimming pool.

"There's some trunks in there." She waved the glass toward a cabana. "Help yourself."

"This isn't a social call."

She took a long drink that emptied her glass, and set it down with a tinkling clatter. "So whadyah want?"

"It's not so much what I want—though I did start out to check some alibis. But the point shifted. It's what Carlo wants."

Marilyn held up a spread hand and one finger. "I know six Carlos."

"This one followed you from the studio today. Carlo Spigotti."

"Spigotti? Am I supposed to know him?"

"You might. He was in business with Derwent."

Marilyn stiffened. She told off Derwent in terms that probably applied to him and ran back several generations. "And this Spigotti! What does he want?" Suddenly fear shivered through her; her big eyes appealed to Pete. "The picture! He's got a dupe negative! Hang it all, Pete, I've paid enough for that crazy episode. Can't you get it away from him? Take it away from him? I've got a gun." She was cat-eager, sensuous and alert.

"Keep it. You may need it. Carlo didn't mention the picture, but he says he knows who did the murders. Or words to that effect."

Marilyn waited, but the eagerness was draining out of her. "What's that to me?"

"He didn't come here?"

"I didn't see him. But I know he's not here now. Jinks has just been around the grounds. With the dogs."

Knowing Jinks and the two dangerous-looking Dobermans, Pete could be pretty sure Carlo wasn't now in the grounds. Then why had he followed first Corliss and then Marilyn? Or had it been Charles he was following?

A bell clattered so brassily from the cabana that both of them started. Marilyn turned to run toward the little frame dressing room, calling lightly over her shoulder, "Phone. . . . Don't go. I want to . . ." She disappeared inside.

Pete waited until she was out of sight and then whipped his long legs into motion. He was beside the cabana in time to hear the rattle of the receiver being picked up, and Marilyn's soft, "Yes?" Then a strident "What!" filled with anger and fear.

She must have held the phone away from her in panicky disgust, for Pete heard the tinny translation of the other voice and recognized it. It was Carlo. "I got it. But the price is cheap this time. And it's the last one. There ain't no more, baby. So you and me can do business. Eleven tonight. Be home, baby." The line went dead. Marilyn said several things before she slammed the phone back into the cradle.

By the time she strode from the cabana she had grabbed up an immense terry cloth beach towel and swathed it around her. She came up to where Pete was pretending he had stayed to pour a martini. She filled a glass, sampled it and nodded approvingly. "Nice."

Marilyn had control of her face and voice now. "Help yourself. There's plenty more. But I have to dress for dinner." She strode away, turned back to smile gayly over her shoulder. "Big night on the town."

Pete could make book on that. Also he would take any side bets on where he'd be from ten-thirty on.

Pete tried through the evening to locate Charles and couldn't, though once he even called Alwyn Phillips who resented it.

"The actor fellow? Drove me home, yes. Didn't stay, no. Seemed anxious to get rid of me, as a matter of fact, after making quite a thing of offering to drive me."

Pete checked back on the hotel and found all was well. Janet came on for a moment and told him not to worry. She was perfectly safe. There were at least eight reporters and cameramen around almost all the time. After that he ate a late, lonely and uninspired dinner and drove back to Canyon Road.

It did him no good. He was crouched outside the Spanish-cum-Gothic monstrosity at ten-thirty, craving a cigarette by ten-forty, desperately wanting a drink, preferably water, by eleven—and aching in every muscle. He had just decided that the guys who wrote books about private eyes were all exceedingly optimistic when he heard the car. Only it wasn't grinding up the last steep incline of Canyon Road. It was starting up, in the big parking circle back of Marilyn's house.

Before he could unhinge cramped muscles it whipped around the house and shot down the drive, turning down Canyon Road toward town, tires squealing.

Carlo had changed his plans. Probably by phone. Pete went back to his car disgustedly, knowing it was no use to try to chase Marilyn now. She had too much of a head start, and less than a quarter-mile away Canyon Road fanned out into half a dozen different roads. Marilyn had slipped her leash.

# 23

After the fiasco of the night before, missing Marilyn and waiting, cold, damp and cramped, until nearly dawn for her to come back, which she did about four a.m., even riding to the studio beside Janet lacked the lift Pete needed.

He was almost surly to the gateman, something rare for him. At the parking lot he let Patsy and Tom escort Janet-Carmen toward the Executive Building while he waited for Jake and Amelia Alwyn, who were trailing in a second studio car.

While he was waiting Marilyn swirled up, driving her modest car, after the newer Hollywood fashion. At least it was modest for Marilyn, but distinctive.

Pete tried to cut through the lot to get to Marilyn, but she was out of the car and tearing toward Stage 7 as if she were late for a shooting schedule. She waved him off, calling blithely, "Can't stop now. See you later." And she slid through the heavy sound-proofed door and closed it behind her.

Before he could go after her, Jake and Amelia arrived, bickering as usual, but it couldn't be serious. Amelia was not yet suggesting she level the studio and sell it off as building lots for bungalows, and Jake had not got around to contemplating the happiness and tranquility of a tailor shop. While he was following them, half hearing the scalding words they were amicably dropping on one another, he saw Charles Abbott drive up and park, and then sit slumped over the wheel, as if he were inexpressibly weary. Pete turned back to speak to him, and Charles suddenly straightened, slid out of the car and scurried almost furtively toward Stage 7, too quickly for Pete to catch him, even for a hurried word. He sighed and went on with Jake and Amelia, up the broad, carpeted stairs to the executive suites. One of them, he was always a little surprised to remember, was his.

An extremely thin, extremely young man got up and beamed over a flat package hugged against his near-Brooks Brothers suit. "Oh, Mister Tobias, I'm so glad I found you. I had that glass replaced." He extended the flat package almost into Jake's astonished face. "And I took the liberty of straightening the frame. I'm George Cavanaugh, from Props."

Jake accepted the package, turning it over in his hands and looking at it blankly, his previous experience with glass being that Miss Fishbein regularly had a pane replaced in the office, how he never knew.

The extremely thin young man gulped nervously. "It's the portrait. You asked me to have it fixed." He cut his eyes around to Amelia. "It's a picture of this lady, I think."

"Nonsense!" Amelia snatched the package and ripped at paper and Scotch tape, tugging the silver frame through a hole obviously too small. Paper shredded away, fluttering down. The thin young man stooped, gathering it up, and then stood looking at Ameba, awed by the glare with which she regarded the portrait.

Her mouth worked several times in advance of words, but when they came their volume made up for the delay. "Jake! Where did you get this?"

Jake leaned to peer over her shoulder. "A camera that can make you look so sweet, I should buy. Then I don't need writers. The camera tells all the lies I need."

"Jake!"

That registered with Jake as genuine anger. He drew back, looking injured. "From that nephew you send out to get in my hair. . . ." He ruffled the scant fringe above his ears.

Amelia stared at the picture, then tucked it under her arm and started briskly down the hall. "Where is he?"

Jake, trotting to keep up, pointed out the door, and Amelia swept through, frustrating Jake's one gallantry, opening doors for ladies. Alwyn Phillips looked up from a stack of papers, scowling. When he saw Amelia he leapt to his feet, his scowl erased in a thin but wide smile. "My dear aunt! I didn't expect you or . . ."

Amelia plunked the picture down face up on his desk and pointed at it. "Alwyn, where did you get that?"

Phillips took a hasty glance at the picture and then turned back to Amelia, ignoring Pete's sidling invasion of the room. "Why, Aunt Amelia." He licked his thin lips, and put out a long, delicate hand to pick up the silver-framed portrait. He smiled over it. "It's a charming picture."

"I asked you, Alwyn, where you got . . ."

Phillips nodded. "I know, Aunt Amelia. And I should have told you I had it." He looked up from a searching study of the picture to smile shyly at Amelia. "It was among Fred's things . . . those things I sent you from Tia Juana. You remember, when I went down there to confirm the rumors of his demise." He took up the picture, opened a drawer and slid the frame into it. "It was the one reminder I had of you." He shut the drawer firmly. "And I intend to keep it." He stood a little straighter, looking directly at her. "I know you don't think much of me, Aunt Amelia, but I'm very fond of you. I know I'm not a demonstrative person. I rarely show my feelings. . . ." He patted the drawer. "But I think I have a right to this. With your permission I'd like to keep it."

"Well!" Amelia looked blankly at her nephew. "If you feel that way, Alwyn, certainly you may keep it."

She blinked and turned away abruptly, hauling at Jake's arm. Pete opened the door and they went on to the hall, Amelia walking with unaccustomed slowness, her long skirts barely rippling. "Maybe I have done the boy an injustice." She sighed softly. "To have kept my picture all these years—and never mentioned it. When he knows . . ." her voice caught, went on . . . "I'd have accepted that picture as proof Fred was gone. I don't believe he'd have parted with it. In spite of the way we quarreled, I adored Fred. And he knew it. Please, Jake . . ." she laid a hand on his plump, short arm . . . "is there some place I could be alone for a few minutes?"

"My office . . ." Jake knew when to be succinct.

Pete watched them going down the hall, then turned into his own office feeling vaguely uneasy. He glanced at the mimeographed sheet of the day's production schedule:

> STUDIO A: Publicity stills; Carmen Merita
> STUDIO 1: Striking sets: "Ladies Will Lie."
> STUDIO 2: Dark
> STUDIO 3: Shooting Scenes #265, 266, 387: "Scrap Happy."
> STUDIO 4: Constructing Sets #14 and 27; "Calais."
> STUDIO 5: Rehearsal, entire company; "Zoomerang."
> STUDIO 6: Retakes, Scenes #189 and 217: "Rampage."
> STUDIO 7: Dark

He paused at that. Studio 7: Dark. Then what the devil were Marilyn and Charles doing in a dark studio? Under other conditions he could have figured that out easily, but with murder and blackmail in the script, he didn't see it as a rendezvous. If he could sneak down there . . .

He slid out of his chair, already feeling furtive, eased his office door open, then closed it to a narrow sliver of a crack and watched Amelia's swift, oddly mechanical locomotion down the hall. In her mittened hands she held a sheaf of papers clutched against her thin, elderly bosom. So Amelia wasn't grieving for her long-dead son in Jake's private sanctum.

After she had passed he stuck his head out and saw her turn in at Phillips' office. He started into the hall and saw her pop out again and continue on down the hall. Although he could see only her back, he got the idea she had lifted the front of her long skirt and was almost running. He waited until she disappeared around a corner and then he stepped into the hall, went as far as Phillips' office and peered in. He got a blinking stare from a startled, spinsterish stenographer—just the sort Phillips would select in a town loaded with beautiful and, in many cases, extremely efficient young women.

"Where's Phillips?"

She fluttered a moment. "That's what she asked. And dumped that stuff on his desk. . . ." She waved a thin, uncertain hand.

Pete looked down at the stuff scattered across Phillips' neat array of books. Papers. Too stiff for papers. He turned one over. It was a glossy blow-up from a single frame, one of the pictures Pete had ordered of Derwent for Fels. He dropped it back. "Where did Phillips go?"

"I don't know," the spinster said wispily. "He got a phone call and just went." A fluttering hand indicated the door.

Pete just went. He headed for the still studio, a great new uneasiness building up. Things had jiggled loose, were falling slowly and uncertainly into an entirely new and ugly pattern.

He brushed past a protesting receptionist and charged into the studio. An elderly man jerked his head from under a square of dark cloth and glared at Pete. "Get out! How can I . . . Oh, it's you." He locked both skinny hands above his head as if he were trying to make sure it stayed on. "How can I make pictures when . . ."

"Where's Carmen?"

The photographer looked as if he wanted to spit. "That female! Coated with goo! Housepaint! Just as soon photograph a barn. Told her to wash it off." He dragged one skinny hand down and pointed. "Dressing room."

He turned back through the curtain and opened a door. No one. He swung across the hall, opening another. He surprised Patsy and Tom in a clinch that would undoubtedly have strangled Phantom. "Hey!"

They broke apart, Tom flushing and patting at Patsy with what was meant to be assurance. Patsy grinned at Pete. "And I thought you were giving us some privacy."

"Where's Ja—Carmen?"

Patsy's grin weakened. "But I just told you . . . I mean, you phoned . . . She was to get her screen test." Patsy's round, plump face screwed up into worry. "You did phone, didn't you?" She hit Tom backhandedly on the chest. "And tell us to wait here?" She caught Pete's slow wag of his head and was pushing by him, trying to get out the door. "She said you wanted her for a screen test."

Pete felt the lurch in his stomach. This was it. And he still didn't know what. "Where? Did she say what studio?"

"She said she was to meet you in Studio 7. She said you'd set up a screen test for . . ."

"Seven is dark." He turned, bolted past the still indignant receptionist, and slammed to a halt against Russell's broad, solid chest.

"You ain't goin' no place. So don't rush." With chest and belly he thrust Pete back into the reception room. "This time you ain't gonna get off so easy."

"Get out of my way, you baboon. I've got to . . ." He saw Bynum Fels' thin face over Russell's shoulder, the oddly virile mustache quivering. "Fels, tell this ape . . ."

"He's got his orders, Mister Hack. To arrest you."

"Arrest me?" Behind and to one side Pete could see Bill Katon, shifting from one foot to the other unhappily. "Your mind—you've lost it! Tell this . . ."

"You were out last night looking for Carlo Spigotti. We found him. Dead. Three bullets from a .22 in him."

Carlo murdered! Pete stepped back, stunned, listening to Fels because his mind refused to work, refused to tell his muscles to lash out at Russell, break through this phalanx in the door and get to Studio 7.

Fels was almost purringly amiable. He suddenly pointed to Patsy. "You, miss. Don't try a break. We've got a warrant for you, too. If you're Patsy Muldoon. And I think you are."

Tom pushed himself forward, and even Russell fell back before the tall Texan's advance. "You cain't talk thataway to . . ."

"And a warrant for you, too. Same charges."

Tom appealed bewilderedly to Pete, looking for instructions and hoping it was the sixth feel so he could go into action. Pete shook his head slightly. A fight now would get them nowhere. He had to think his way out of this one. And quick.

Fels' voice was going on. "And we're catching up with other tricks you've pulled, Mister Hack. That Mexican red herring—she never came from Mexico. She got on the plane at Yuma. We got the plane's manifest. And that other smoke screen you're throwing out. Amelia Alwyn. Checked on the plane at Yuma, too. The real Amelia Alwyn is at death's door in New Jersey. I just talked to her doctor. I don't know what you thought you'd gain by . . ."

Pinwheels spun inside Pete's head, exploded into wild, impossible designs, and then settled into something real and utterly horrible. He swallowed hard. "Will you let me go if I give you Janet West—and the murderer?"

"Rat!" It was Patsy's voice, harsh, hard, all laughter gone.

Pete could see Bill Katon's broad, homely face twist in disgust and he felt rather than saw Tom's horrified withdrawal. But there wasn't time to explain. He had to stop another murder.

"She's on Stage 7." He brushed once more against Russell's bulk and heard Fels' sharp order. Russell grudgingly gave way and Pete leaped through the door. "This way." And he spun down a tight iron spiral of stairway. "Short cut!" After that he saved his breath, putting it into pumping his legs faster. At the small, flat iron door he fumbled for what seemed like long, endless minutes before he remembered it slid on a track instead of opening inward. He rolled it back and plunged into the vast, dark vault of Studio 7.

At first the deep, sound-proofed silence of the huge dark cavern settled down like an almost palpable blanket. Then he saw the dimly lighted segment in the far corner, and heard sounds of movement, swallowed up in the noise of feet pounding along behind him. With that noise there was no need to attempt secrecy. He rushed across the great, barren room, stumped his toe on a huge, snake-like cable and plowed stumblingly on, fighting for balance. He righted himself and careened on, around a projecting wall of scenery.

And stopped.

In an old set, only partially dismantled, the lights were on, showing up mercilessly the cracked plaster, dust, limp coils of rope, an overturned chair, a settee stacked with tired artificial plants. And a tiny figure that moved with smooth, oddly mechanical precision around the edge of a doorway, partially hidden by shadows from lights turned toward the plaster-and-lath facade of an Italian villa. The face was tilted up at a sharp angle, and one hand went up, pointing. And in it Pete could see the glint of metal on a gun.

He looked up the steep face of the mock Italian villa, squinting against the glare of lights. And then he saw her, pinned by the glare, a slim colorful figure, high on the fight bridge, the gaudy peasant outfit gleaming against the dark above and behind.

Janet!

# 24

Behind him Pete could hear the others, coming more cautiously now, so that the noise of their approach was almost lost in the sound-absorbing walls. He started forward, ducking, running low, across the fringe of the lighted stage. He saw the sliver of wood leap up at his feet before he heard the flat, thin slap of a gun from high on the light bridge. He swerved, ducking farther out of the light, headed for the slender, tiny figure half crouched now behind the door. Even as he ran, he saw the hand move, a flash, and then heard the dull splat of the gun.

From the bridge he heard a scream, high, thin, womanish. As he ran, he swung his head around and saw Janet sag, slumping down, saw her hands grabbing at the thin metal rail. She went down on her knees, swayed sideways and almost fell from the high steel bridge.

The tiny figure, seeming even tinier against the massiveness of the set, raised the gun again.

"I'll kill you!"

And fired. The bullet whanged into something metal high up, whined off in a ricochet and thudded against a wall.

Pete looked up, watching, horrified, as Janet's fingers seemed to be slipping from the rail, her gay, colorful figure, pinned with light, sagging under the slim steel bar, crumpling into space with forty feet of nothing below—and then the concrete floor. He wasn't too familiar with Studio 7, but somewhere off to the left he remembered a spider-thin ladder climbed to the light bridge. If he could get up that . . .

It meant crossing in front of the tiny figure with the gun. Without looking—somehow it seemed easier if he didn't know for sure the bullet was coming—he heaved into the light, running low, weaving as he'd been taught in a long-ago war, aiming for a black rectangle of darkness in the mock wall. In his crouching run he saw it happen.

Bill Katon must have circled well outside the light, moving swiftly and silently for such a heavy man—as Pete knew he could. He saw Bill's scoop-shovel hand swoop out of the dark, engulfing the pistol, wrapping the tiny figure to him. They both seemed to vanish, tumbling out of the edge of light into the blackness beyond the set, just as dust spat where they had been and another bullet whined off—to thud into a sound-proofed wall. Then he heard the curiously flat spat of the gun, high on the light bridge.

He heard the scuffle of sound where Katon and the tiny figure had vanished and a high, tiny, enraged voice screaming, "You fool! Let me go! I'm going to kill . . ."

Still weaving, Pete risked another glance at the light bridge. From this angle he could barely see her, just the bright splash of her skirt and the silky shimmer of a knee. Then he saw the flash of the gun beside her, felt the searing rake of the bullet along his arm, the numbing thud as it creased his elbow and then the blinding pain. Pain meant he wasn't dead, didn't it? He staggered, caught himself, and lunged for the door.

Then he heard the voice from the bridge, sharp, high, tight with hysteria.

"Don't move or I'll shoot!"

Lousy dialogue, Pete thought crazily. Worse than Tom's horse operas. But there was a quality of command under the desperation. Pete took another staggering step and righted himself, standing still.

"Don't anyone move, or I'll shoot the girl—first."

Far-off and lost in the sound-proofed cavern, he heard Patsy cry out, and then, closer, Tom's deep, booming oath. Idiotically Pete catalogued that as the first swearing he'd ever heard from the Texan.

"You can't get away with this!" Fels' voice came from somewhere out of the dark, sounding oddly peevish, as if he weren't quite certain it was true.

"I'm taking the girl with me."

Now Pete could see him, foreshortened by the great height, thick, solid, almost squat, so different from the slender, precise Alwyn Phillips he had known. And like an extension of one angled arm, he could see the glint of light along the barrel of the gun pointed down at Janet sprawled awkwardly on the slender metal treads of the light bridge.

He could hear Phillips ordering her to get up, hear the scrape of her feet, the thin tinkle of a bracelet. Then he saw the knee withdrawn and the bright edge of skirt receding, pulled onto the light bridge as she stood up. He could see the gleam of one white hand clasping the slender rail.

"Janet!" Pete called her name involuntarily.

"I'm all right." It was shaky and thin but somehow not frightened.

Now he could see them both standing on the narrow steel scaffolding not more than three feet apart, the gun pointed at Janet's blouse.

"We're getting out of here." Phillips' voice was shrill, quavery. "And nothing happens to the girl . . . if nothing happens to me." He was reading third rate melodrama badly, only this was for real, with Janet's life at stake. "I'm taking a car. The girl's driving." It was quick, breathed gustily. "So both my hands are free. Don't anyone move."

Fels' voice echoed his, this time with authority. "Don't anyone move." Then he aimed it at Phillips. "You can't get away with this, Phillips. We'll get you, you know. Give up now and make it easier for yourself."

"Easier? How?" Phillips snickered hysterically. "A pad in the electric chair?"

Pete was aware of a soft susurration of movement separate from the feet sliding and shuffling along the steel walk overhead, but he didn't dare turn his head to look, aware that Phillips was staring over the rail at him. Lighted from below, Phillips' face looked gauntly Mephistophelean, twisted with hate. His mouth worked.

"I should have killed you! The stupid police . . ."

Pete knew what the movement was now. Out of the tail of his eye he saw him, moving with almost Indian quiet into the light. Tom Brady! His great white hat was like a suddenly sighted beacon.

Stop him! Somebody stop the fool! Pete's throat ached with the words he didn't dare speak aloud. He eased his head around, hoping to mouth something at Brady that would halt him.

"Phillips!" Brady's powerful voice cracked sharply in the sound-proofed room. Quick, harsh, without echo.

Phillips whipped around, slanting the gun across the rail, snapping a shot at the white target.

There was a blur of motion. Both of Brady's guns were out, belching and cracking. And in another instant they were back in their holsters and Brady was striding forward.

Still half turned, Pete looked up. The gun in Phillips' hand was drooping tiredly. It slid from his slack fingers, clanged against steel and caromed off into the dark. Phillips' knees buckled slowly. For an instant his chin hung on the rail; then his head snapped back and he pitched through the rail, cartwheeling down through the light, to thud soddenly on the concrete floor.

Katon wheeled out of the shadows, gun drawn, but even as he came up to Phillips he was thrusting it away. He glared at Brady. "That was a fool thing to do! He mighta shot the girl!"

Brady looked down at Phillips, shaking his head. "Uh-uh, podner. A man always figgers he's gonna shoot at something special, but when there's danger, he shoots at the danger. It's like instinct. I've been a sheriff. I know." He looked up, smiling shyly. "A real sheriff. Not just in pictures."

Katon nodded, accepting this with the same simplicity he had accepted all of Tom Brady. "And that was real fast drawing." He looked momentarily blank. "Always thought it was faked. . . ."

Pete heard most of that on his way up the spidery stairs to reach Janet. She met him partway down. It was a little cramped and things were slightly confused, what with him trying to comfort Janet and Janet trying to assure herself he wasn't mortally wounded. But, cramped and awkward as it was, it was very pleasant.

Alwyn Phillips looked up at them with strangely calm eyes. He frowned in mild surprise. "I don't hurt."

Katon nodded. "You don't feel it. Neck's broken." He said matter-of-factly, "You're dying. Want to say anything?"

Phillips ran his eyes over the faces ringed above him, reading the truth, and sighed. His eyes sought out Amelia Alwyn's. "I really thought he was dead. Then he turned up here. As Edgar Derwent."

Amelia put out a mittened hand, withdrew it. "You didn't tell him I had forgiven him? That he wasn't disinherited?"

Phillips' mouth set stubbornly, lips thinned. "I couldn't. It meant giving up everything. Besides," he went on peevishly, "he wanted everybody to think he was dead. He arranged it all down in Tia Juana. It even fooled me. For nearly three years. Until he showed up. He wanted money and introductions. Everything went all right until Carlo heard about the reward you offered, for information about him. They'd been partners—or something—down in Tia Juana. Carlo told Derwent about the reward. From that he figured you had forgiven him, and he was going home. He planned to ditch Carlo and let me drop." His thin lips twisted. "Back to being the poor relation again. I couldn't take it. For three years he wanted to be dead. So I just helped him out." His mouth twisted in a sudden surge of pain—or regret. "I brought my own gun—a target .22—but one of his looked so much more efficient." Yes, even at a time like that Phillips would think of efficiency. "He saw me and grabbed at me. He got the .22 from my pocket. So I had to shoot him then. It was self-defense. He actually shot at me." Phillips scowled at Fels. "That does make it self-defense, doesn't it? I mean, his shooting at me."

Pete frowned, remembering the nude with the extra navel. "He missed."

Phillips agreed sourly. "He was drunk. Celebrating. When I was losing everything. I left the gun I shot him with right beside him." He peered accusingly at Fels. "You were supposed to think it was suicide. I took my own gun."

Fels gnawed at his moustache. "Well, the girl took it."

"Oh, yes. The girl. At first I thought she was a good thing. A break. Everyone was so sure she was guilty."

Fels had the grace to flush and turn away from Janet.

"Only it wasn't a break. Mister Hack kept interfering. It would have been so much nicer if . . ."

"What about Germaine Winters?" Fels turned attention from his blunder over Janet.

Phillips frowned in annoyance. "She knew I had got Derwent on as an extra. And besides, she was friendly with him. He might have told her something. So I poisoned her whiskey. Women shouldn't drink." He said it pettishly and then looked at Fels. "You know, it's criminal how careless they are with poisons in the labs. I just walked in one day and pretended to look around—and took some." He sighed. "Only it didn't kill her. That Struthers girl—just an accident." As if it were somehow Fels' fault. "After that you had Miss Winters. And Pete was going to ask her the very question that would ruin me. So I got her out. In his name, of course."

"You went to see her?"

"Oh, yes. As head of the studio, I called on her for information. She was quite ready to talk, but she hadn't associated me and Derwent yet. She was rather stupid, you know. But if somebody had asked her the right questions . . . So I shot her." He puckered up his mouth angrily. "It was really self-defense, you might say." Phillips was quite capable of justifying his murders.

Katon growled deep in his throat, and Fels waved him to silence, watching Phillips. "And Carlo Spigotti?"

"A very low person, Mister Fels. A criminal, really. I don't understand the type. He was quite willing to make a deal over the death of his friend. Blackmail, really. That's what it amounted to." Phillips frowned perplexedly. "In some ways a rather astute person. He apparently hadn't been aware of Derwent's or Andrews', as he had known him, real identity until he learned about the fingerprints on the ransom note. He was able to couple that with the reward you offered and figure things out." Phillips' voice faded to a whisper. "He had the audacity to suggest a partnership."

"How did you find him?"

Phillips frowned, gathering some last remnants of strength. "He found me. He'd been following me all day."

So it had been Phillips, not Corliss or Marilyn or Charles, that Carlo had been after.

"We went for a drive. He wasn't afraid of me." Phillips looked up, suddenly wide-eyed. "He rather regarded me as a joke. He doesn't now."

"And why were you going to kill the girl?" Fels nodded to Janet in the circle of Pete's good arm.

"She'd seen the picture of Aunt Amelia. I heard her mention it. At the hotel. There was only one. He'd kept it." He stared up at Amelia, glaring, as if he wanted to hurt her. "Not out of affection, but as proof of who he was. It was the only one. If I had it, it would prove he was dead. And I'd get the money." He smiled up into the blazing lights, with eyes now blind. "All that lovely money . . ." His mouth sagged open and his head lolled loosely. He was dead.

Fels blinked down at the sprawled, twisted figure. "Picture? Proof of who he was?" He snapped his up, glaring around at them. "Who was he? This Derwent, I mean?"

"My son. Fred Alwyn." Amelia said it quietly and started to turn away.

"But . . ." Fels looked at her perplexedly. "You're not Amelia Alwyn. She's in West Long Branch, New Jersey, dying. I consulted her doctor."

Amelia turned back, looking at him with mild contempt. "I hope he charges you twenty-five dollars for the consultation. That's what he charges me. And he always thinks I'm dying. It makes it so much more impressive when he cures me of a cold."

"But the plane manifest! There wasn't any Amelia Alwyn listed. Except from Yuma."

"Young man," Amelia made it sound almost infantile, "when I want to get away I never make reservations in my own name until I'm too far for that walking stethoscope to do anything about it."

Fels backed off a step, taking a new and less aggressive stance. "If Derwent was your son, Fred Alwyn, why . . ."

He spread his hands helplessly, laying open the whole question.

Amelia took Jake's proffered arm. Just where the little producer had come from or when he had arrived Pete didn't know, but he was beside Amelia now, his round face grave and solicitous. Amelia gave him a wisp of a smile and turned back to Fels. "My son was difficult. Unbridled. And I'm afraid I gave him very little discipline, and far too much money. It's so easy to ruin those we love. He went wild and ran up heavy gambling debts. I put on the brakes—too late, refusing him any more money. And he became desperate, though I didn't know it. Then he was kidnapped. I paid a five hundred thousand dollar ransom, and he came back. I suspected right away that he had engineered it himself. I understand fingerprints on the ransom note have since been positively identified as his, but I knew, without proof. I told him then I was going to disinherit him, and he ran away. My nephew, Alwyn Phillips, as you know, undertook to find him. And he did. In a horrible place in Tia Juana. Or at least proof that he was dead. You heard him. He really believed it." Amelia's rose-petal face crumpled. "I can't understand why my son wanted to be thought dead."

Pete could. As he watched the group breaking up and the police officials taking over, he began to think about it. Undoubtedly Fred Alwyn had kidnapped himself to get money from his mother to pay his gambling debts. The gamblers Fred would have been dealing with could make it exceedingly unhealthy if he didn't. But once he had the money—and found himself disinherited—he had undoubtedly decided disappearing into Mexico with the cash was better. But it probably hadn't been good enough, and retribution was catching up, and the money had been squandered. So he had "died" to rid himself of his Nemesis. Davey Petry's suicide could easily have given him the idea and, with a few minor bribes, the "death" was arranged. In Carlo's company he must have learned many of his blackmailing tactics and been reasonably content, until he learned that perhaps he wasn't in such disgrace at home. Letting Phillips know he intended to resume his rightful place had been his mistake. Phillips had been the heir apparent to the Alwyn millions too long to give it up. And that had started a chain of murders. Now it was over.

Pete turned to stare at Janet, frowning. "Get that make-up off. And wash out that hair dye." He took his arm away so hurriedly Janet staggered. "And you shouldn't be hanging around a publicity man. You're going to be a star." He handed her over to Patsy and a thoroughly bewildered Tom. "Take her to Hammond. He'll fix her up." Pete pushed her resolutely into Patsy's arms.

Patsy hugged her close, glaring over Janet's soft bare shoulder at Pete. "For a very bright boy you're awful dumb."

Pete watched them go, puzzling over Patsy's remark. Finally he shrugged. He still had a job to do. He slid around the bustle of activity on the lighted set and made his way to a rank of dressing rooms along the far wall. He moved along them, listening, until he heard a whisper of movement. He opened the door and slid in, without turning on a light, and spoke into the darkness. "You can come out now. You don't have to worry about Carlo. He didn't have Derwent's blackmail material."

He heard the sigh and then Marilyn's voice. "So you guessed why we sneaked in here. I knew you saw us. Charles and I were frantic when he didn't keep his appointments. . . ."

"Carlo was busy keeping a very permanent appointment. He's dead. Now go out and prove you're actors. Be properly horrified. Phillips is the killer."

Under the cover of Marilyn's horrified gasp and Charles' hoarse, frantic whispers, he slid out, walking toward the small door that led to the executive suites and his office.

Fels had been using Jake's office—by a mild maneuvering he was unaware of—to clear up the last details of the case. He rose to leave, waving a slim hand in salute to Pete and Jake. "You've been very co-operative. Finally. Now I must go out and talk to the press." His oddly virile moustache bristled importantly. "They'll want a complete statement from me on a case like this—full of important Hollywood names."

Jake propped his head in his hand and moaned. "Even dead that Phillips is a headache. Now in a tailor shop . . . Pete, I got headaches. I got worries like I never had before. Amelia gives me the studios. It's my own money I'm flinging away now. Listen. . . ." He pointed dramatically to the immense electric clock on the wall. "Every time that clock ticks, Loeb Films is costing me maybe five hundred dollars."

"But it doesn't tick," Pete pointed out truthfully.

"Does that cut expenses?" Jake buried his head in his hands for a moment and then looked up. "Pete, how is it suddenly you know the truth? Down there in the still studio." He held up a pudgy hand suddenly. "No. Don't tell me on company time. It costs me money even to listen to you."

Pete grinned, then worried over it himself. How had he known? It had all just slipped into place. The trigger for the chain reaction had been Amelia's picture. And the fact that, at the hotel, Janet had mentioned recognizing Amelia from a picture. Despite Amelia's statement that she looked like all old ladies of seventy, she was too much an individual for that to have been the truth. And there had been a big silver frame among "Derwent's" missing effects. And one had turned up in Alwyn's hands. It tied things together. Then he shoved his hat back on his head, banged the heel of his hand against his forehead. I should have known from the very beginning it was Phillips. There in the projection room, when the news came through, I didn't say how Derwent died—but Phillips said "shot." And then he said the police had been very clever, solving a murder within four hours of its being committed. How had he known when it was committed? He felt Jake's eyes on him and glanced at his boss.

"You are finding maybe you are a dumbkopf?"

Then Jake's round face lit up. He stood up, holding out both hands to someone behind Pete. Without turning Pete knew it was Janet. He decided he wouldn't turn.

He turned, looking at her. Gone was the sultry beauty of Carmen Merita, over-rouged mouth and artificially black hair. This girl was simple, soft and compellingly lovely. Pete gulped. He managed to wave a hand at her, not too steadily. "Well, Jake, you got your star back."

"Oh, Pete . . ." Janet was walking toward him, lovely, wide-eyed, young. "You've been wonderful. . . ."

"You're going to be a star," he said unsteadily.

"A star?" Jake's voice bellowed. "Out of tears and tragedy maybe I make a star. But with a face full of love! Who can make a star of that?"

Before Pete realized it, Jake had whisked out of his office and shut the door, leaving Janet standing there beside the huge desk. She looked eatable. Pete felt his throat working. Then he heard Jake, talking to Miss Fishbein outside.

"And they're getting married and going to have six kids." The door popped open and Jake's head came through. "But only between pictures."

# About the Authors

Douglas Stapleton was born Samuel Granville Staples (1907-1972), growing up in Virginia. (In the 1950s, his mother is referred to as Mrs. H. C. Link of Virginia Beach, so the 'Harry Link' in this book's dedication might be Douglas' stepfather). Douglas Stapleton may have started out as a pen-name, but appears to have been taken on for most professional use. According to one newspaper article, Stapleton "started out as a song-and-dance man with Eleanor Powell in her first success, 'The Wedding of the Painted Doll,' became historical correlator for the *Encyclopedia Britannica*, advertising man with General Foods, program manager for a radio station and radio commentator and (in Washington) administrator for the W.P.A. and later Radio Expert for the executive office of the president." After service in the naval reserve and teaching at the Ft. Monmouth signal corps O.C.S., he worked as an advertising executive in New York for a wide variety of TV and radio programs. As an author, Stapleton wrote a multitude of books, articles, short stories, radio plays, and television comedies.

It was while working in New York that he met and married his third (?) wife, Dorothy, in 1941. Dorothy Tucker Aden (1917-1970) was from Bastrop, Louisiana, where she had worked as a political speechwriter, theatrical company

press agent, licensed engineer, radio station operator, film director and producer, and creator and writer for the army radio serial, 'This is Your Judge Advocate.' She moved to New York to become director of radio, TV and films for Grey Advertising, where she met Douglas. While on their honeymoon, they co-produced a Broadway play, 'Questionable Ladies,' and wrote their first novel together, *The Corpse is Indignant*. For this, and only this mystery, Dorothy used the pen-name Helen A. Carey. In future collaborations, the pair went by Douglas and Dorothy Stapleton. They continued to work together on radio shows, monthly magazine columns, and other projects. *American Magazine* called them "the people who work 48 hours a day." (For relaxation, they both obtained their pilot's licenses.) They 'retired' to Virginia Beach in 1951, becoming involved in community work and some further mystery writing for Arcadia House (*Late for the Funeral*, *Corpse and Robbers*, and *The Crime, the Place, and the Girl*). This retirement didn't last long, as they had moved to Monroe, Louisiana, in 1953 to help operate a new radio station, though it shut down the next year. Their mystery novel writing ended after the mid-1950s (though short stories for mystery and science fiction magazines were published into the 1960s), and both Douglas and Dorothy appear to have lived their final years in Los Angeles, California.

LATE
for the
FUNERAL
Douglas and Dorothy
Stapleton

CORPSE
AND
ROBBERS
Douglas and Dorothy
STAPLETON

A JUDGE MASSIE
MYSTERY
THE CORPSE IS
INDIGNANT
DOUGLAS STAPLETON
and HELEN A. CAREY

WHISPER MURDER!

VERA KELSEY

Also Available
Coachwhip Publications
CoachwhipBooks.com

BLOOD-RED
DEATH
MINNA BARDON

The Railroad
Murder Case
R. M. LAURENSON

The Case of the
Six Bullets
R. M. LAURENSON
239
F40FH
239

www.ingramcontent.com/pod-product-compliance
Lightning Source LLC
LaVergne TN
LVHW090942080826
845145LV00003B/852

* 9 7 8 1 6 1 6 4 6 5 7 3 5 *